LISTEN WITH MOTHER

LISTEN
WITH MOTHER

With an introduction by
Sir Harry Secombe

Illustrated by Douglas Hall

First published in 1992 by Cresset Press
an imprint of the Random Century Group Ltd
20 Vauxhall Bridge Road, London SW1V 2SA

Printed by Cox & Wyman Ltd, Reading, Berks

ISBN 0 09 175410 0

Contents

Introduction   7
  Sir Harry Secombe
I can squash elephants!   9
  Malcolm Carrick
The higgledy piggledy house   13
  Eugenie Summerfield
Gary the Greatest   18
  Margaret Joy
The Flippy Floppy Man   22
  Rachael Birley
Simple Simon and the fiddler's tune   27
  Jean McKenzie
Stanley and the band   31
  Marjorie Newman
The cat's in the apple tree and won't
  come down   36
  Anne Wellington
Mr Baboon discovers a new animal   42
  David Chilton

Little Pig Perkins looks for a good
   home   47
  Elizabeth Robinson

Simon Rhymon   50
  Shelley Lee

Father Christmas and the seaside
   outing   54
  Ann Das

Special Percy   58
  Margaret Stewart

Mrs Minniver's shopping   63
  Anne Wellington

Wriggly Worm and the Evil Weevil   67
  Eugenie Summerfield

Dad's cough and the peculiar plant   72
  Judith Drazin

Thomas and the Monster   75
  Marjorie Stannard

King Greenfingers and the giant
   rhubarb   80
  Gordon Snell

The pale purple pullover   84
  Emma Milton

Archie the singing donkey   88
  Ann Burnett

Lazy Witch to the rescue   92
  Eleanor Tims

Introduction

Once upon a time when I was younger and lighter and had a lap, I would place the youngest of my progeny on it, check the time, turn on the radio at 10.30 a.m. and breathe a sigh of contentment. 'Are you sitting comfortably?' the voice would say. 'Yes,' we would both reply. 'Then I'll begin.' Oh, what transport of delight would flow from the speaker of our Grundig portable, whilst in the armchair by the fire Jennifer or Andrew or David or Katy and I would sit entranced, not moving until the story was done. Opposite us in another armchair my wife would snore happily. We used to call this time of day 'Listen without Mother', because it was about the only chance she had to rest from the constant demands made on her, and she cherished every second of it.

In countless households across the country a similar peace would reign – a fifteen-minute armistice in the constant battle between parent and child for supremacy. Indeed, the threat of not being allowed to 'Listen with Mother' was enough to guarantee a truce in our house. The stories themselves were always stimulating and often inspired interesting questions from my children. Questions like 'Why can't you read to us like that, instead of doing all those silly voices?' I could never answer that one. There's an art in reading stories to children.

Now, thanks to Hutchinson, I have the opportunity to read the stories from 'Listen with Mother' to my grandchildren; that is, if they will allow me to do so. They seem to have inherited my own children's aversion to my silly voices. Perhaps I should start with 'Wriggly Worm and the Evil Weevil' or perhaps 'Mrs Minniver's Shopping'. Let's have a go anyway. 'Now are you sitting comfortably? Then I'll begin. . . .'

Sir Harry Secombe

I can squash elephants!

Malcolm Carrick

Are you sitting comfortably? Then I'll begin.

Once there was a hare who had a house shaped just like a funnel. And one wet night a caterpillar crept into Hare's home, out of the rain, and wiggled all the way to the back of the house. The next morning when Hare awoke he was surprised to find funny tracks running to the back of his house.

'Who's there? Who's in Hare's house?' he called.

Caterpillar was frightened and said, 'IT'S ONLY ME.' His voice came booming through the house, because, like a megaphone, it made it louder. Hare jumped and ran outside, in terror of the loud voice.

Caterpillar saw how he had frightened Hare and thought, 'What a mighty animal I must be. I could squash elephants!'

'I CAN SQUASH ELEPHANTS!' he boomed.

Hare jumped back, and ran a little way from the door, and bumped into Fox.

'Oh Fox,' he said, 'there's a dangerous fierce animal in my home. Can you get him out for me?'

Fox sniffed into the entrance of Hare's home.

'Who's that?' Fox said. 'Who's in Hare's home?'

'ME!' Caterpillar yelled. 'The fiercest animal in the world, I can squash elephants.'

Fox went back to Hare. 'I'm sorry, Hare,' he said, 'I'm not brave enough to go in there, you'd better find somebody braver.'

Hare thought for a moment and decided to go and see Tiger. When he found him in the jungle, he explained about the fierce animal in his house so Tiger said, 'I'll come and see what I can do.'

When they got to Hare's house, Tiger puffed out his huge chest and bellowed, 'Who's there? Who's in Hare's home?'

'ME!' Caterpillar replied. 'I'm the fiercest animal in the whole world, and I can squash elephants!'

Tiger wasn't as brave as Hare had thought.

'I'm not going in there, Hare. If he can squash elephants what can he do to tigers?'

So Tiger bounded back into the jungle.

Hare sat down and thought. 'Oh dear, what can I do?' Then he felt the ground go bump, bump. 'I know who that is,' he thought. 'Of course, the one person who can help me. Elephant,' he called. 'Elephant, come and help me won't you?'

Elephant plodded up. 'What seems to be the trouble, Hare?'

'There's a fierce animal in my home, he says he can squash elephants.'

'Does he now?' said Elephant, and putting his trunk into the entrance he trumpeted, 'Who's that? Who's in Hare's home?'

'ME!' cried Caterpillar. 'I'm the fiercest animal in the whole world – I can squash elephants.'

Elephant pulled his trunk out of the house and ran off, shouting back to Hare, 'You'd better run away from here, I'm not going to stay around and be squashed.'

Hare was beside himself. Everybody was frightened of the fierce animal in his house, there was nothing he could do, he would have to find somewhere else to live.

'Maybe I can help you,' said a croaky voice behind him. Hare turned round and saw it was

11

a fat old frog.

'You?' said the Hare, 'You? What can *you* do, you're only a frog.'

'Well I'll try anyway,' Frog said. And the old frog croaked into the hare's house, 'Who's that? Who's in Hare's house?'

'ME!' yelled the cheeky caterpillar. 'The fiercest animal in the world. I can squash elephants.'

Hare waited for Frog to run away at the fierce voice, but much to his surprise, Frog leapt right to the back of the house.

'You're only a caterpillar making your voice echo,' said Frog. 'Hop it.' And Caterpillar did: out of the back door as fast as he could.

So Hare found out who was in his home after all.

The higgledy piggledy house

Eugenie Summerfield

Are you sitting comfortably? Then I'll begin.

Down upon the sea shore there was once a higgledy piggledy house.

'No matter how hard I try,' said the house, 'I can't stand up straight.'

Its windows sloped this way. Its doors sloped that way. Its ceilings were all sagging and its floors weren't flat.

Now on sunny days the higgledy piggledy house was happy. Children came down to the sea shore. They came over the red rugged cliffs. They had picnics and played on the smooth sand. Sometimes they paddled in and out of

13

the sea.

But when it was cold and wintry, when the wind blew, when the sky was grey and the sea was inky black, no children came. No one came except the grey sea gull. He always stopped to rest on the higgledy piggledy chimneys whenever he was flying that way. He told the higgledy piggledy house stories about the other houses in the country and the town.

He was there one misty moisty morning when the higgledy piggledy house cried, 'Oooh, I am so sad.' Great black sooty tears ran down the chimneys.

'I'm all alone!' sobbed the higgledy piggledy house. 'No one loves me.'

'Well, I like you,' squawked the sea gull. 'I like the way your windows slope this way and your doors slope that way, your ceilings all sag and your floors aren't flat. And there must be lots of people who love higgledy piggledy houses like you.'

But the higgledy piggledy house went on crying. So the sea gull said, 'Now listen, you're no ordinary house. And I'm sure you can do anything you want to do.'

The higgledy piggledy house straightened up a bit, thought for a moment and said, 'Then I'd like to move. I'd like to go to some of the places you've been, in the town and the country.'

'Today's the day,' called the sea gull. 'There's a swirly curly fog coming in from the sea. It's just the day for magic and mystery.'

The swirly curly fog was spreading all over the sea shore, and all over the red rugged cliffs. The higgledy piggledy house pulled itself up as straight and as tall as it could and off it went. Up over the cliff tops, away down the long road, and after a while the higgledy piggledy house found itself in front of some very grand iron gates.

Beyond the gates was a smooth white drive and on each side were flowers of all colours.

'Oooh,' sighed the higgledy piggledy house, 'This is the place for me. I'll stay here.'

The higgledy piggledy house was tired. There were blisters on its humpy bumpy floor boards and its sagging ceilings ached.

The higgledy piggledy house settled down to rest.

Now it wasn't very long before the rich man whose drive it was, came home. And when his golden car nearly crashed into the higgledy piggledy house in the swirly curly fog, the rich man was very angry.

'What's that higgledy piggledy heap of bricks doing in my drive?' he roared. 'Clear it away at once.'

So the higgledy piggledy house set off to find another place to stay.

Over the fields, through the long cool grasses, the higgledy piggledy house went until it came to a farmyard. Horses, cows, pigs and hens lived there.

'This is where I'll stay,' said the higgledy piggledy house.

But as soon as the animals saw the higgledy piggledy house they began to shout and snort, to squawk and squeal.

Higgledy piggledy house was very sad.

'Now, now,' clucked a kindly old hen, 'Go down to the town. That's the place for a house like you.'

Higgledy piggledy house raced away down the road, past the police station, past the post office and the supermarket round the corner and then . . .

'Why this *is* the place for me,' cried the higgledy piggledy house. There, all in a row, were higgledy piggledy houses, and there was a gap just big enough for the higgledy piggledy house to squeeze into.

Hardly anyone noticed the next day when the swirly curly fog had gone that there was one more higgledy piggledy house than there used to be. Except a higgledy piggledy man who said, 'Why that's just the house for me and my higgledy piggledy family.'

So they all moved in. And sometimes the grey

sea gull came to rest on the higgledy piggledy chimneys when he was flying that way.

And they all lived happily ever after.

Gary the Greatest

Margaret Joy

Are you sitting comfortably? Then I'll begin.

There was once a Strong Man called Gary the Greatest. He worked at a fair.

Every day he put on his shiny red shorts, his white vest, and his boxing gloves. He stood on a platform in front of the crowd and shouted, 'Roll up, roll up! Come and watch me, Gary the Greatest! Watch me lift tremendous weights above my head! Watch me bend iron bars! You have never seen anyone as strong as me.'

The people would look with goggle eyes as Gary flexed his mighty muscles and lifted enormous weights. Then they would cheer and throw money onto his platform.

Sometimes Gary would shout, 'Ladies and Gentlemen! I will give a Super Prize to anyone who can beat me at weight-lifting, or bending iron bars. No one has done it yet. Gary is the Greatest!'

Sometimes men would jump up onto Gary's platform and try to lift his weights, or bend his bars.

But there was a big gong over Gary's platform and before they had even lifted them from the ground the gong would sound, DOOOOING!

And Gary would say, 'Time's up.' And their chance would be over! 'No one has ever won my Super Prize,' Gary said. 'I can beat anyone!'

Then one day a little old lady called Miss Maisie was at the fair. She was having a lovely time. She had been on the roundabouts three times. She had been in the Hall of Mirrors. She had been on the Ghost Train. Now her purse was quite empty!

'Listen to that Strong Man shouting!' she said. 'I wish I could beat him.'

She stood and watched Gary for some time, then she said, 'Hi! Mr Gary the Greatest, hi!'

She was so little Gary didn't see her at first. Then he saw she was right in front of him.

'Did you want me ma'am?' he said with a grin. 'Perhaps you would like to try for the Super

Prize? Ho, ho, ho,' he laughed. And all the crowd laughed too.

'Why that is exactly what I was thinking,' Miss Maisie said. 'I think I have something you won't be able to lift. It's in my handbag.'

Gary the Greatest was so tickled when he heard this that he laughed and laughed and laughed.

'Well, ma'am,' he said, 'If you have anything in that old handbag that I can't lift, I promise to give you that Super Prize. Ho, ho, ho! Perhaps you'll make quite sure my gloves are tied really tight,' Gary said. 'I want to be quite sure I am ready for this tremendous weight-lifting, ho, ho, ho!'

So little Miss Maisie tied up the laces of his boxing-gloves as tightly as she possibly could.

Then Gary started to shout again, 'This little old lady says I can't pick up something in her handbag! Hold up your handbag, ma'am.'

Miss Maisie held up her old black handbag.

'Now, are you still sure you mean it, ma'am?'

'Yes, oh, yes,' said Miss Maisie.

'Right then,' said Gary. 'Put the object on my platform.'

Miss Maisie opened her bag, and carefully placed A PIN, an ordinary pin, in the middle of the platform.

With a great laugh Gary bent down and tried

to pick it up. Then he tried again. He wasn't laughing any longer. He tried again.

But he had his great gloves on, firmly tied by Miss Maisie and he couldn't get hold of that tiny pin!

He knelt down. He crouched. He lay on his stomach and blew the pin along the ground . . . .

Then – DOOOOING! The gong went. Miss Maisie's pin was still lying on the platform.

Gary the Greatest groaned. Then he handed Miss Maisie a ticket.

'You have won. You have certainly won my Super Prize! It's a ticket for free turns on anything here at the fair. You can stay all day and it *won't cost you a thing*.'

Miss Maisie had a wonderful day at the fair. She had free goes on everything!

After that day she always kept a pin in her handbag. 'You never know when a pin will come in handy,' she said.

The Flippy Floppy Man

Rachael Birley

Are you sitting comfortably? Then I'll begin.

There was once a little girl, and one afternoon it was raining and she was bored. So she went to her Dad and said, 'What can I do?'

'Ah,' said her Dad, 'I know what you can do.' And he got out of the cupboard a pair of scissors, a packet of felt tips and some paper. Then he got out of the drawer some bendy paper clips.

'We are going to make a Flippy Floppy Man,' he said.

First of all he took the paper and cut out a shape like a leg, and gave it to the little girl to colour. Then he cut another shape like a leg and two shapes like arms. The little girl coloured the first leg shape red and the second leg shape blue. Then she coloured the two arm shapes yellow.

'Here is his body,' said Dad, 'and here is his head.'

The little girl coloured his body green and then gave him orange hair and a nice smile on his face. They fixed his red and blue legs, and his yellow arms and his smiley face all on to his green body with the paper clips; and the little girl held him up by the top of his yellow hair. There he was, a Flippy Floppy Man. And she played with him till bed time.

When she went to bed, she put the Flippy Floppy Man carefully on the table by the window. Then she went to sleep.

The Flippy Floppy Man didn't feel a bit like going to sleep. The table was hard and he could see, through a gap in the curtains, that it was still light outside.

'It's much too early to go to sleep on a nice fine summer evening,' he said to himself. 'I'm going to have a look around, on my first evening in the world.' So he got off the table and went quietly out of the room. Naughty of him, wasn't it? But he had only just been made and he did want to see what was what.

23

The Flippy Floppy Man went out of the front door, being very careful not to let it bang behind him. It had stopped raining and Dad was cleaning the car. He didn't see the Flippy Floppy Man. But the cat did.

'Miaou,' said the cat. 'What are you doing out here?'

'I've come out to see what's what,' said the Flippy Floppy Man.

'Someone,' said the cat, her eyes gleaming dangerously, 'might think you were a mouse and try to catch you.'

'Catch me if you can, I'm a Flippy Floppy Man,' cried the Flippy Floppy Man, and he ran off as fast as the wind blows a leaf over the ground. The cat sat down, and started to wash herself.

The Flippy Floppy Man ran down the road until he came to a big red something standing at the edge of the pavement. It was smooth, and quite shiny, and round. He stopped and looked at it, and then walked round it several times, but he couldn't find a way in. Just then a dog came by.

'Woof,' he said. 'What are you doing out here?'

'I've come out to see what's what,' said the Flippy Floppy Man. 'Can you tell me what this red thing is?' He gave the dog his best and most polite and nicest smile, because it was quite a large dog.

'That,' said the large dog, 'is a pillar box. People post letters in it. Someone,' he said, thoughtfully, 'might think you were a letter, and post you into it. I should think it would be very dark inside.'

'I don't think I'll wait for that to happen,' said the Flippy Floppy Man, and away he ran, shouting, 'Catch me if you can, I'm a Flippy Floppy Man.'

The dog sniffed at the pillar box and walked off.

The Flippy Floppy Man ran on and on. He kept to the pavement because of the cars on the road, and now and then he went round a corner, but the pavement always went on ahead of him. His legs got tired and his feet hurt.

'I wish I'd stayed at home,' he thought.

He turned another corner and saw a little brown bird sitting on the fence, watching him.

'You must be getting tired,' said the little brown bird sympathetically.

'I am,' said the Flippy Floppy Man.

'You've run right round the block three times,' said the bird. 'That's a lot of running. Not even the little girl can do that, and she's much bigger than you.'

'Right round the block?' said the Flippy Floppy

Man. 'Do you mean I've been going round and round in circles?'

'Yes,' said the bird.

'Then I must be nearly home?'

'Yes,' said the bird.

'Hurrah,' said the Flippy Floppy Man. 'Because, "all Flippy Floppy Men must be in bed by ten", and I thought I was going to be late. Goodnight, little bird, I'm going to go in now, and go to bed.'

'Goodnight, Flippy Floppy Man,' said the little brown bird. 'Sleep well.'

Simple Simon and the fiddler's tune

Jean McKenzie

Are you sitting comfortably? Then I'll begin.

One morning as Simple Simon was going to the fair he met, no, not a pieman this time, but a fiddler. This fiddler was wearing a green suit and a green hat with a feather in it and as he walked along he played a merry tune.

'Good morning, Mr Fiddler,' said Simon politely, 'that's a very nice tune. Would I be able to play it if you lent me your fiddle?'

'I expect so,' said the fiddler, 'but be careful. The tune might fly away as it isn't used to you.'

Simon looked at the fiddler quickly in case he was pulling his leg, but he wasn't laughing. His

27

face was very serious.

'Here you are, young man,' he said, and he gave his fiddle and the bow to Simon. Simon took hold of the fiddle very carefully, and tucked the fat end of it under his chin. Then he scraped the bow across the string.

'Ugh,' said the fiddler, 'what a disgusting noise. Try again.'

Simon tried again and this time, there was the same *scrape* but after that came a horrible *twang* as the string broke.

'Oh, my goodness,' cried the fiddler, 'now you've done it, the tune's got away. I said it would.'

Simon looked round but, of course, you can't *see* music, you can only hear it. But he couldn't hear a thing except the birds twittering.

'You'll have to find it,' said the fiddler, 'I can't go to the fair without a tune. I shall go to sleep under this hedge until you bring it back.' And down he lay.

Poor Simon was in a fix. He stood in the country lane and listened. He could still hear nothing except the twittering of the birds. Then, from the distance, he heard the sound of church bells. But he could not hear the fiddler's tune.

Then he saw a shepherd coming towards him.

'Oh, please, Mr Shepherd,' cried Simon, 'I've lost the fiddler's tune. Have you heard it?'

'Why, no,' said the shepherd, 'I've only heard my new born lambs bleating in the fields over there. Listen.'

Simon listened and he could hear the baby lambs in the distance. But he could not hear the fiddler's tune.

The shepherd went on his way and next Simon met a woodcutter.

'Oh, please, Mr Woodcutter, I've lost the fiddler's tune. Have you heard it?'

'Why, no,' said the woodcutter, 'I've only heard the wind rustling in the trees. Listen.'

Simon listened and he could hear the trees rustling their leaves, but he could not hear the fiddler's tune.

The woodcutter went on his way and Simon saw a fisherman sitting by a stream nearby.

'Oh, please, Mr Fisherman, I've lost the fiddler's tune. Have you heard it?'

'Why, no,' said the fisherman, 'I've only heard the water rippling over the stones. Listen.'

Simon listened and he could hear the water as it rippled over the stones, but he could not hear the fiddler's tune.

He sat down sadly by the water's edge, wondering what to do. Then he heard the cuckoo as she flew out of a wood nearby.

'Cuckoo, cuckoo, cuckoo.'

'That's not the fiddler's tune,' he thought and

then, suddenly, he realized what had happened.

'I'm a cuckoo,' he said, 'I've let the fiddler pull my leg. The string has broken. You can't play a tune on a fiddle with a broken string.'

He got up and ran back to where the fiddler lay asleep under the hedge, his green hat over his eyes. Simon tiptoed up and carefully took the feather out of the cap and began tickling the fiddler's nose with it. The fiddler sat up quickly.

'Wh-a-a-t are you doing? Ahhchoo!'

'I'm tickling your nose because you pulled my leg about the fiddle,' said Simon. 'You can't play a tune on a fiddle with a broken string.'

'You can't play it anyway if you don't know how,' said the fiddler, and they both began to laugh.

'Come on,' said the fiddler, 'I'll mend the string.'

So he mended the string on the fiddle and began to play.

'Oh, what a lovely tune,' said Simon happily, and he and the fiddler went off to the fair together.

Stanley and the band

Marjorie Newman

Are you sitting comfortably? Then I'll begin.

Stanley, the big, brown dog, stood at the corner of the village street. Stanley's ears were pricked up. He was listening.

The village band was coming! Stanley's big brown tail began to wag. He loved listening to the band.

Now Stanley could *see* the band! The band came marching round the corner, with Mr Higgins the band-leader in front.

Stanley could see the trumpeters; and the tambourine players; and the drummers; *and* Joe, who played the big bass drum. Stanley's tail wagged very hard. He stood and watched the band march past.

Stanley stood and watched until the band had gone right down the road, and round the corner. He stood listening, until he couldn't hear it any more.

Then Stanley went home. He sat in his dog bed (which was made from a large cardboard box), and he thought. He thought about the village band. 'I wish I could play in the band,' he thought.

And then – he had an idea! It was such a good idea that Stanley's big, brown tail began to wag against the side of his cardboard-box bed. Thump, thump, thump, went Stanley's tail.

'What I must do,' said Stanley to himself, 'What I must *do*, is go down to the village hall on Tuesday, when they're having their band practice, and ask Mr Higgins the band-leader if I can be in the band! He's sure to say Yes!'

So, on Tuesday evening, Stanley went out of his house and down the road to the village hall. As he got closer, he could hear the band practising.

Stanley's tail began to wag with excitement. He rushed up to the door of the village hall, pushed it open with his nose, and went in.

'Woof!' said Stanley. 'Woof, woof, woof!' And he ran over to Mr Higgins the band-leader, and stood with his tail wagging.

'Hallo there, Stanley!' said Mr Higgins. 'What *d'you* want, then?'

'Woof, WOOF, WOOF, WOOF, WOOF!' said Stanley.

''E's worked up about *something*!' said Joe, from behind his big, bass drum. 'What's the matter, boy?'

'WOOF, WOOF, WOOF, WOOF, WOOF!' said Stanley.

'Now then, now then!' said Mr Higgins. 'Less of that barking! We're having a band practice! Can't you see?'

'WOOF, WOOF, WOOF!' said Stanley.

'Stanley!' said Mr Higgins. 'Unless you lie down and keep quiet, you'll have to go.'

Stanley's ears drooped, and his head drooped, and his big, brown tail drooped. Stanley wanted to be in the band – not lie down and keep quiet!

'You be a good dog!' said Mr Higgins. 'There's no need to look so sad, Stanley.'

''Ere, Mr 'Iggins!' said Joe, putting down his big bass drum. 'Ain't it time for our tea-break?'

Mr Higgins looked at the clock on the wall.

'So it is!' he said. 'Take ten minutes, lads.'

So all the bandsmen put down their instruments, and went out to a little room at the back of the hall for a cup of tea and a chat. Stanley was left on his own.

When he was sure no one was about, Stanley tiptoed over to one of the trumpets, which was lying on a chair. Stanley put his mouth to the trumpet, and tried to blow. PFFFFFFFFFFFFFF! PFFFFFFFFFFFFFFFF!

'Oh dear!' said Stanley. 'That's no good. I can't play a trumpet.'

He looked around. Then he tiptoed across to a tambourine which was lying on a chair. He put up one of his paws – and tapped the tambourine. CLATTER, CRASH! The tambourine fell to the ground. Stanley jumped back – right against a chair with another tambourine on it! CLATTER, CRASH! *That* tambourine went spinning to the ground!

''Ere!' cried the bandsmen, running back into the hall. 'What's going on?'

Stanley wagged his big, brown tail very fast. He was very sorry he'd knocked the tambourines down. He hadn't meant to.

'Stanley!' cried Mr Higgins, pushing his way through to the front of the crowd. 'Stanley! What's the idea?'

Stanley lay down, still wagging his big, brown tail, to show how sorry he was. Thump, thump, thump it went on the floor of the hall.

'Knocking down the tambourines!' scolded Mr Higgins.

''Ere!' cried Joe. 'I believe old Stanley wants to

be in the band!'

Stanley sprang up, and ran across to Joe, and licked Joe's hand; because Joe had guessed exactly right. The bandsmen roared with laughter.

'A dog play in a band!' they laughed.

Stanley got excited. His tail wagged harder than ever. He was standing right by Joe's big, bass drum which was all ready for Joe to pick up. Stanley's tail thumped against the drum. BOOM, BOOM, BOOM! it went.

''Ey up!' cried Joe. 'Listen to that all of you.'

So the bandsmen stopped laughing, and listened to Stanley's tail going BOOM, BOOM, BOOM on the big, bass drum.

'Reckon he *could* play in the band!' said Mr Higgins.

'Will you let him have a go, Joe?'

'Of course I will,' said Joe.

Then the bandsmen picked up their instruments – all except Joe. He picked up one of the small side drums, instead of the big, bass drum. Stanley stood with his tail ready.

Then the band played. And Stanley, the big brown dog, played with them!

The cat's in the apple tree and won't come down

Anne Wellington

Are you sitting comfortably? Then I'll begin.

Old Mrs Fussle had a little black cat. And she made such a fuss of the little black cat that he couldn't be a cat by himself for a moment.

'Eat up your fish,' she would say. 'Drink your milk. Never talk to strange dogs. Be careful where you walk. And never climb a tree, never, never, never, or you might fall out of it and break your little back.'

The little black cat got so tired of all the fuss that he climbed up an apple tree, to be there by himself.

Mrs Fussle saw him, and she said, 'Dearie me!
Come along down, Pussy Black, Pussy Black.
Come along down or you'll break your little back.'

But Pussy Black stayed where he was in the tree.
'I'm a cat by myself,
By myself in a tree.
Which is just where a cat by himself
Should be.'

Old Mrs Fussle ran along the road till she saw Mr Wellbelove watering his beans. She said, 'Mr Wellbelove, will you come and help me? The cat's in the apple tree and won't come down.'

Mr Wellbelove said, 'I'm watering my beans.' But he went with old Mrs Fussle just the same.

They stood beneath the apple tree looking up and calling,
'Come along down, Pussy Black, Pussy Black.
Come along down or you'll break your little back.'

Some rain spattered down from a big black cloud, but Pussy Black stayed where he was in the tree.
'I'm a cat by myself,
By myself in a tree.
Which is just where a cat by himself
Should be.'

Old Mrs Fussle ran along the road till she saw Mrs Honeybone hanging out her washing. She said, 'Mrs Honeybone, will you come and help me? The cat's in the apple tree and won't come down.'

Mrs Honeybone said, 'I'm hanging out my washing.' But she went with old Mrs Fussle just the same.

They stood beneath the apple tree looking up and calling,
'Come along down, Pussy Black, Pussy Black.
Come along down or you'll break your little back.'

The sun came out from behind a cloud, but Pussy Black stayed where he was in the tree.
'I'm a cat by myself,
By myself in a tree.
Which is just where a cat by himself
Should be.'

Old Mrs Fussle ran along the road till she saw Mr Patterson picking red plums. She said, 'Mr Patterson, will you come and help me? The cat's in the apple tree and won't come down.'

Mr Patterson said, 'I'm picking red plums.' But he went with old Mrs Fussle just the same.

They stood beneath the apple tree looking up and calling,
'Come along down, Pussy Black, Pussy Black.
Come along down or you'll break your little

back.'

A breeze came blowing, and it rustled through the leaves, but Pussy Black stayed where he was in the tree.
'I'm a cat by myself,
By myself in a tree.
Which is just where a cat by himself
Should be.'

Old Mrs Fussle ran along the road till she saw Mrs Clutterbuck calling home her chickens. She said, 'Mrs Clutterbuck, will you come and help me? The cat's in the apple tree and won't come down.'

Mrs Clutterbuck said, 'I'm calling home my chickens.' But she went with old Mrs Fussle just the same.

They stood beneath the apple tree looking up and calling,
'Come along down, Pussy Black, Pussy Black.
Come along down or you'll break your little back.'

The sun went down a pink and orange sky, but Pussy Black stayed where he was in the tree.
'I'm a cat by myself,
By myself in a tree.
Which is just where a cat by himself
Should be.'

Mr Wellbelove, and Mrs Honeybone, and Mr Patterson, and Mrs Clutterbuck stood beneath

the apple tree and looked at Mrs Fussle.
'Well, Mrs Fussle, the cat is in the tree.
He won't come down for anyone, as anyone can see.
So, Mrs Fussle, we hope we shan't offend you,
But we've all got business of our own to attend to.'

And they all went home along the road.

Mr Wellbelove's beans had been watered – by the rain. Mrs Honeybone's washing had been dried – by the sun. Mr Patterson's plums were blown down – by the breeze. Mrs Clutterbuck's chickens had come home to roost, because they had seen the sun going down.

So *that* was all right, but dearie me! Pussy Black was still in the tree.

The sky behind the tree grew as black as Pussy Black was, so old Mrs Fussle couldn't see him any more. She only saw the stars, and she said, 'That's peculiar!
However can this be?
The cat's *not* in the tree
As far as I can see.
Oh dearie dearie me!'

And she went indoors. There was nothing else to do.

A big yellow moon came up behind the tree, and Pussy Black yawned, and stretched his legs. 'I'm a cat by myself,

By myself in a tree.
I won't come down for anyone
As anyone can see.
A cat by himself
Is a cat that is free.
The only way that I come down
Is by myself you see.'

With a slither and a scramble and a long leap downwards Pussy Black landed on the grass beneath the tree. Then he walked across the garden and went home to eat his supper.

Mr Baboon discovers a new animal

David Chilton

Are you sitting comfortably? Then I'll begin.

Once upon a time there was a little monkey called Mr Baboon. He belonged to a little girl called Isobel, and he slept in the toy cupboard in Isobel's room along with all her other toys.

Now the main thing about Mr Baboon was his curiosity. He was a very curious little monkey and he loved exploring.

One day he climbed all the way up the long staircase and along a narrow passage until he came to the room at the top of the house. This room was all blue like the sky. It had blue curtains and blue walls, and in one corner there was a big blue cupboard.

It was this cupboard that Mr Baboon had come to explore. Very carefully he reached up with his long hairy arm and opened the door. To his surprise he found himself face to face with the strangest creature he had ever seen. It was a small hairy sort of animal which reminded him a bit of Isobel's little brother, but it was altogether more peculiar.

'Hooo, Hooo, Hooo,' went Mr Baboon, hastily shutting the cupboard door.

'A new animal,' he thought to himself, 'I must find Big Bernie.'

Big Bernie the Teddy Bear was downstairs in the kitchen thinking about tea time.

'Come and look, Bernie,' said Mr Baboon, arriving all out of breath. 'There's a strange animal in the blue cupboard upstairs.'

'All right,' said Big Bernie, 'let's have a look.'

Big Bernie and Mr Baboon clambered up the stairs and along the passage.

'Be careful!' whispered Mr Baboon as they stood in front of the big blue cupboard. 'I'll open the door, and you stick your head round and have a look.'

'All right,' said Big Bernie. And he did. 'Ooooer.'

'Did you see it?' asked Mr Baboon.

'Cor yer!' said Big Bernie, 'A strange new

animal . . . 'Orrible.'

'We'd better go and find Pink Elephant,' said Mr Baboon.

'All right,' said Bernie. And off they went.

Pink Elephant was very old and wise, and knew all sorts of things about all sorts of things. They found him in the kitchen sink bathing himself and blowing bubbles in the water with his trunk.

'Ahem,' said Mr Baboon politely.

Pink Elephant pretended not to notice and went on blowing bubbles.

'Ahem,' said Big Bernie.

'No questions today,' said Pink Elephant, and he suddenly sucked up lots of water in his long trunk and squirted it all over his back.

'We've found a new animal,' said Mr Baboon. 'Yer,' said Big Bernie, 'a new animal.'

'Describe it,' said Pink Elephant.

'What?' said Mr Baboon.

'What?' said Bernie.

'What did it look like?' sighed Pink Elephant.

'Oh it was small and hairy,' said Mr Baboon.

'No, no, it was large and furry,' said Big Bernie, 'and 'orribly ugly.'

'Well, not very ugly,' said Mr Baboon.

''Orribly ugly,' said Big Bernie.

'I wish you'd make up your minds,' said Pink Elephant, flapping his ears with impatience.

'Well, maybe it was small and hairy but in a large furry sort of way,' said Mr Baboon.

'That's preposterous,' said Pink Elephant, and he disappeared under the water.

'Ah,' said Mr Baboon.

'Ah,' said Big Bernie, and off they went to find Isobel.

'So that's what it is,' said Mr Baboon, 'a preposterous!'

'I wonder what they eat,' said Big Bernie.

Isobel was in the drawing room, drawing. 'Come and look at the preposterous,' said the two animals.

'What?' said Isobel looking up from her drawing.

'It's a new animal. Bernie and I found it in the blue cupboard. Pink Elephant says it's called a preposterous.'

'Nonsense!' said Isobel, 'there's no such thing.'

'But I've seen it,' said Mr Baboon.

'Yer, so have I,' said Big Bernie, ''orrible looking thing.'

'Very well,' said Isobel, 'I suppose I'd better come and look.'

And they all went upstairs, Isobel, the small hairy Baboon, and the large furry Teddy Bear. When they got to the cupboard Isobel opened the door very carefully and looked inside.

'Did you see it?' asked Mr Baboon.

Isobel started to laugh. 'You clowns,' she said, 'there's nothing in here but an old mirror – you've been looking at yourselves!'

She opened the door of the cupboard ever so wide and there they *all* were in the mirror: Isobel, the small hairy Baboon, and the large furry Teddy Bear.

'Do I *really* look like that?' said Mr Baboon.

'Cor,' said Big Bernie.

Little Pig Perkins looks for a good home

Elizabeth Robinson

Are you sitting comfortably? Then I'll begin.

There was great excitement in the farmyard.

'The farmer's wife has found a good home for Miss Purr's kitten,' crowed the Rooster.

'I would like to go to a good home,' said Little Pig Perkins.

'Piglets don't go to good homes,' said Mrs Pig. 'They stay on the farm.'

But Little Pig Perkins didn't want to stay on the farm. He wanted to be like Miss Purr's kitten, and go to a good home.

On the next fine day, Little Pig Perkins set off to look for a good home. He came first to a white cottage, and knocked on the door. It was opened by an old woman.

'Please, would you give me a good home?' Little Pig Perkins asked the old woman.

'If you can catch mice, I will give you a good home,' said the old woman, who had mice in her pantry.

'I can't catch mice,' Little Pig Perkins said sadly.

'Then I can't give you a good home,' said the old woman.

Next to the white cottage was a pink bungalow. Little Pig Perkins knocked on the door. It was opened by an old man.

'Please, would you give me a good home?' Little Pig Perkins asked the old man.

'If you can make treacle toffee, I will give you a good home,' said the old man, who liked treacle toffee.

'I can't make treacle toffee,' Little Pig Perkins said sadly.

'Then I can't give you a good home,' said the old man.

Soon Little Pig Perkins came to a wood. In a clearing in the wood stood a caravan. On the steps of the caravan sat a gypsy.

'Please, would you give me a good home?' Little Pig Perkins asked the gypsy.

'If you can sing and dance, I will give you a

good home,' said the gypsy, who needed someone to sing and dance to his music.

'I can neither sing nor dance,' Little Pig Perkins said sadly.

'Then I can't give you a good home,' said the gypsy.

'I will try one more time to find a good home,' said Little Pig Perkins to himself. He walked on until he came to a thatched cottage. There were geraniums flowering in pots on the window sill, and at the back of the cottage was a large garden. In the garden a man was planting potatoes.

'Please, would you give me a good home?' Little Pig Perkins asked the man. The man's back ached from digging holes for his potatoes.

'If you can dig holes for my potatoes, I will give you a good home,' he told Little Pig Perkins.

'I can't catch mice, I can't make treacle toffee, I can neither sing nor dance – but I *can* dig holes,' said Little Pig Perkins joyfully.

All the rest of that day Little Pig Perkins dug holes for the man's potatoes. At tea-time the man took Little Pig Perkins into the cottage. There, sitting by the fire, was Miss Purr's kitten.

'Come along in,' she told Little Pig Perkins, 'And make yourself at home.'

Simon Rhymon

Shelley Lee

Are you sitting comfortably? Then I'll begin.

There was once a boy called Simon Rhymon who lived at the top of a block of flats. There were ever so many flights of stairs to reach up to Simon's flat, so most people took the lift.

Not Simon! He didn't take the lift! He liked to go up the stairs and up the stairs and up the stairs and up the stairs to find his mother at the top.

'Just pop down to the shop, Simon,' said his mother, 'and buy a pot of honey.'

So Simon ran down the stairs and down the stairs and down the stairs and down the stairs and along the street to the shop. On the way he sang to himself, 'A pot of honey. A pot of honey. A lot of money. A lot of money.'

When he got to the shop he was in such a muddle! He asked the shopkeeper for a lot of money!

'Get along with you, Simon Rhymon,' said the shopkeeper. 'I can't give you a lot of money. We don't sell money here!'

So Simon went home along the street and up the stairs and up the stairs and up the stairs and up the stairs to find his mother at the top.

'The shopkeeper says he doesn't sell a lot of money,' he told her.

'Oh Simon Rhymon!' said his mother. 'I'd better go myself.'

Now the next day Simon's mother said, 'Pop down to the shop and buy a slice of cheese.'

So Simon ran down the stairs and down the stairs and down the stairs and down the stairs and along the street to the shop. On the way he sang to himself, 'A slice of cheese. A slice of cheese. A hive of bees. A hive of bees.'

When he reached the shop he was in such a muddle! He asked the shopkeeper for a hive of bees!

'Get along with you, Simon Rhymon,' said the shopkeeper. 'We don't sell bees here.'

So Simon ran home along the street and up

the stairs and up the stairs and up the stairs and up the stairs to find his mother at the top.

'The shopkeeper says he doesn't have a hive of bees,' he told her.

'Oh Simon Rhymon,' said his mother. 'I'd better go myself.'

Now the next day Simon's mother said, 'Pop down to the shop and buy a pound of pears.'

So Simon ran down the stairs and down the stairs and down the stairs and down the stairs and along the street to the shop. On the way he sang to himself, 'A pound of pears. A pound of pears. A mound of bears.'

When he reached the shop he was in such a muddle! He asked the shopkeeper for a mound of bears!

'Get along with you, Simon Rhymon,' said the shopkeeper. 'We don't sell bears here.'

So Simon ran home along the street, and up the stairs and up the stairs and up the stairs and up the stairs to find his mother at the top.

'The shopkeeper says he doesn't sell bears,' he told her.

'Oh Simon Rhymon,' said his mother. 'You are a silly boy. Your head can't remember anything for two minutes. You had better get yourself another head.'

So Simon ran down the stairs and down the stairs and down the stairs and down the stairs and along the street to the shop. On the way he sang to himself, 'I'll buy myself another head. I'll buy myself a loaf of bread.'

When he reached the shop he was in such a muddle he asked the shopkeeper for a loaf of bread.

'Certainly Simon,' said the shopkeeper, and gave him a loaf of bread.

So Simon ran home along the street and up the stairs and up the stairs and up the stairs and up the stairs to find his mother at the top.

'The shopkeeper sold me a loaf of bread,' he told her.

'Thank you, Simon,' she said. 'That's just what we needed for tea today. How did you guess?'

Father Christmas and
the seaside outing

Ann Das

Are you sitting comfortably? Then I'll begin.

Mrs Crighton-Wobblegood looked after Father Christmas's toy factory.

Every year, soon after Christmas, the gnomes checked the machines, the elves repainted the workshops and the fairies tidied up.

Then Father Christmas locked the factory and went to visit his brother at the South Pole; and everyone else went on holiday. Mrs Crighton-Wobblegood got out her skis and flew to Switzerland. She liked skiing in Switzerland, but she longed to go to the seaside and build sandcastles.

'Why can't we have Christmas in August?' she

asked Father Christmas one day.

'Because it's in December,' he reminded her.

Mrs Crighton-Wobblegood thought it was a great pity, but there was nothing to be done. So she thought of a summer holiday by the sea, sailing and swimming all day, 'And building sandcastles,' she added aloud.

'What are sandcastles?' asked Father Christmas.

'Well . . .' said Mrs Crighton-Wobblegood. 'You make them at the seaside, and the tide comes in and eats them up, and it's great fun.'

'Oh!' said Father Christmas. It was so long since he had been to the seaside that he had forgotten all about sandcastles and paddling and sitting on the beach eating ice-cream.

'Suppose,' he said much later when he had thought about it, 'we all go to the seaside for the day. We could take a picnic – crisps and sandwiches, and jellies and things. And we can borrow buckets and spades from the toy-store.'

So that is exactly what they did.

While the gnomes rounded up the reindeer and harnessed them to the sleigh, the elves found the buckets and spades and the fairies packed the picnic lunch.

As soon as they were all ready, Father Christmas locked the toy factory and hung up a big notice: 'CLOSED FOR STAFF OUTING TO THE SEASIDE.'

Then everybody climbed on the sleigh and Father Christmas shouted, 'Away . . . away!'

In no time they arrived at the seaside and unharnessed the reindeer who trotted off to play among the waves.

First the elves went swimming and the gnomes sailed a boat. The fairies looked for shells and Mrs Crighton-Wobblegood took off her shoes and stockings and had a lovely paddle.

They were so busy that they forgot about sandcastles.

After the picnic Father Christmas sent the gnomes to get ice-creams. While they were eating them he asked Mrs Crighton-Wobblegood to tell them about sandcastles.

'I've a better idea,' she said. 'I'll show you how to make one.'

And she did. It had towers and walls, turrets and a moat all the way round.

'My, that's beautiful!' said Father Christmas.

'We'll never be able to make them as well as that,' announced the elves.

'Of course you can, and better,' Mrs Crighton-Wobblegood told them.

So they all took buckets and spades and went off in little groups to build sandcastles. But, it was already getting late.

'We'll have to go home soon,' thought Father Christmas. The tide was turning as he finished his third strawberry lolly.

Mrs Crighton-Wobblegood and Father Christmas decided the sandcastles were all so good that everybody deserved a prize.

'Look!' shouted Father Christmas, 'The sea's come to eat them all up!'

And sure enough the waves were lapping at the walls of the castles.

Then everyone started clearing up the picnic. The gnomes harnessed the reindeer and Father Christmas got more lollies for prizes; and finally they all climbed into the sleigh to go home.

'That *was* a lovely day,' said Mrs Crighton-Wobblegood when they were outside the factory again.

Father Christmas agreed. 'It *would* be nice to have Christmas in August,' he said, 'but as we can't we'll have an outing to the seaside every year instead.'

And they do. So, if you see reindeer galloping in the waves when you are building sandcastles, you will know that Father Christmas is somewhere near, enjoying his day by the sea.

Special Percy

Margaret Stewart

Are you sitting comfortably? Then I'll begin.

'Well, Percy, I am very sorry,' said Joe the bus driver, as he backed Percy into the garage. 'This is your last trip. The bus company have decided to use the new, small buses in future. They are very smart and don't need so much looking after. So, as they say that you are rather old and shabby you can't work any more.'

'In fact,' Joe went on, 'I don't think that I will want to work on these new buses either. I am getting too old. I think that I will just stay at home and look after my garden.'

Percy was very upset. He had known that he was getting old. That he would soon have to stop working. But, really – to be replaced by one of those snooty, cheeky, single-deckers. To be just left in the garage to grow shabbier and dirtier every day. That was a terrible thing to happen.

But happen it did and Joe retired to his little cottage. There he grew flowers and vegetables. Yet in spite of having retired, Joe and Mrs Joe did not forget Percy. Twice a week they called down to the garage and cleaned and polished the lonely bus. They swept out all the dirt and cobwebs. They shooed out the birds, who kept trying to build nests in Percy's engine. Then they would shine the windows and start the engine to make sure it did not stick.

Percy looked forward to these visits. He did not like being left alone in the dusty garage. He was very grateful for all this attention. He liked to look clean and shining even if his seats and paintwork were rather shabby.

Even so, most of the week, Percy was left alone in the garage and he hated it. He had only the birds, spiders and mice to talk to. He liked them all very much, but he missed going out each day. Mostly he missed Joe and his passengers.

However, one day, to Percy's surprise, Joe

came to see him unexpectedly. It was not his usual day and he had Mrs Joe and two strangers with him.

They walked round and round Percy, talking quietly to each other. Then they went inside and walked down between the seats. After this they did the same thing upstairs.

At last, 'That's great, Joe,' the older man said. 'I am sure that we can use it again. We must go now and get the plans working.'

Both men went out of the garage with Joe, leaving Mrs Joe behind. She was very excited.

'Oh, Percy, what a lovely surprise,' she said. But she did not say what the surprise was. She just patted his bonnet. She then rubbed a duster over his headlights and went out after Joe and the strangers.

Soon after this Joe brought more strangers to the garage; men wearing white coats. The fore-man walked round Percy. Then he stood and scratched his head.

'Yes, Joe, we will make a good job of your bus,' he said. 'Right lads, let's get to work.'

'The bus is called Percy,' Joe answered. 'He and I are good pals and we have travelled many miles together.'

'Well,' said one of the workmen, 'when we have finished, Percy will be ready for the road again and you will both travel many more miles together.'

Poor Percy, the men were all over him. They pulled out all his seats. He could not work out what they were trying to do. But each evening Joe stayed behind and talked to him.

'Don't worry too much, Percy,' he said. 'I know that it all looks dreadful now, but you will soon look lovely again. Just trust me.'

So Percy stopped worrying and trusted Joe, while the men pulled out his lights and seats. They took away the luggage rack and the conductor's shelf, under the stairs.

Soon, all the taking out was finished. Then the men began to paint and decorate inside and outside of Percy. All his inside walls were painted the beautiful, clear yellow of a buttercup. While all around the windows they painted a sparkly white.

Outside, instead of dark green, they painted Percy as blue as the summer sky. All around, large pictures, pictures of Mickey Mouse and his friends, birds and butterflies flew right across the roof. Lastly, right across the front, over Joe's driving cab, they painted the words that told everyone just what Percy was.

PERCY, THE NEW PLAY SCHOOL BUS

Soon, one lovely sunny morning, Joe and Mrs

Joe came to the garage to see Percy.

'Well Percy, Mrs Joe and I are both going to work on you from now on. I will drive as before. Mrs Joe's job will be helping to look after the children who will use you.'

So, now Joe and Mrs Joe take Percy out every day (except Sunday when they all rest). They drive all round the villages. They go to a different one each day. Whenever they come into sight the village children gather round and cheer Percy, as they are so pleased to see him.

Percy is delighted to be working again. He is really proud of his shiny self. He does not mind at all, being the only double-decker bus around.

After all he is *special*, isn't he?

Mrs Minniver's shopping

Anne Wellington

Are you sitting comfortably? Then I'll begin.

Old Mrs Minniver said to herself, 'I shall take my basket on wheels up the hill to Mr Moggs the grocer and do my bit of shopping.' But old Mrs Minniver couldn't find her shopping list. She said, 'Oh well, I'll remember in my head.
A fresh green lettuce,
A slice of pink ham,
Some tea to fill the caddy up,
A pot of strawberry jam,
And I hope no one talks to me, else I shall forget.'

Further up the hill she met a small brown dog.

'Woof, woof! I've nowhere to live,' said the dog. 'Can I come and live with *you*?'

And he jumped in the basket. Old Mrs Minniver went on up the hill, with the small brown dog in the basket.

'Now, what was on my shopping list again?' she said.

'A fresh green lettuce,
A slice of pink ham,
Some tea to fill the caddy up,
A straw of potty jam.'

Further up the hill she met a little black cat.

'Miaow! I've nowhere to live,' said the cat. 'Can I come and live with *you*?'

And she jumped in the basket. Old Mrs Minniver went on up the hill with the dog and the cat in the basket.

'Now I mustn't forget my shopping list,' she said.

'A fresh green lettuce,
A slice of pink ham,
Some tea to cad the filly up,
A straw of potty jam.'

Further up the hill she met a little red hen.

'Coopy, coopy! I've nowhere to live,' said the hen. 'Can I come and live with *you*?' And she jumped in the basket.

Old Mrs Minniver arrived at the grocer's, with the dog and the cat and the hen in the basket.

Mr Moggs the grocer said, 'Good morning Mrs Minniver. What's on your shopping list today?'

Mrs Minniver told him, 'I couldn't find my shopping list. I had to remember it in my head today.

A fresh pink lettuce,

A slice of green ham,

Some tea to cad the filly up,

A straw of potty jam.'

Mr Moggs said, 'You're all mixed up, Mrs Minniver. In any case, your basket is full up already, with a dog and a cat and a little red hen.'

Old Mrs Minniver said, 'So it is. I'd better take them home, and come back with my shopping list.'

When she got home, *there* was the shopping list, tucked behind the clock on the mantlepiece. Old Mrs Minniver put it in her pocket. She said, 'Little dog, little cat, little hen, stay here at home while I go and do my shopping.'

Up and up the hill went old Mrs Minniver, and into the grocer's and she said to Mr Moggs, 'Now Mr Moggs, here is my shopping list.

A fresh green lettuce,

A slice of pink ham,

Some tea to fill the caddy up,
A pot of strawberry jam.
   And now with extra mouths to feed, I've
thought of three more things I need.
Some dog food for my little dog,
Some fish to feed my cat,
A bag of corn to feed my hen,
And that, I think, is that.'
   Down and down the hill went old Mrs
Minniver. When she got home the small brown
dog was standing by the gate, guarding the
house. The little black cat was just inside the
door, mewing to welcome Mrs Minniver home.
The little red hen was waiting in the kitchen.
   She had laid a fine brown egg, on the doormat.
Old Mrs Minniver smiled, and she said, 'That's
the best day's shopping I've ever, ever done.'
   She gave the dog his dog food. She gave the
cat her fish. She gave the hen her corn. And then
she had her tea. Some fresh green lettuce and a
slice of pink ham. A fine brown boiled egg, and
buttered toast with jam. And two cups of tea to
finish up with!

Wriggly Worm and the Evil Weevil

Eugenie Summerfield

Are you sitting comfortably? Then I'll begin.

'Wriggly Worm! Wriggly Worm!'

It was the little Brown Snails calling. They sounded rather upset.

'What's the matter?' asked Wriggly Worm, as the little Brown Snails crowded round him.

'It ... it's that *thing*, over there,' cried the smallest of the Brown Snails.

'It's that Evil Weevil. He's in our playground and he's causing trouble. We're afraid to play there any more.'

Then all the Brown Snails cried very loudly.

'Oh, he is, is he? I'll soon settle him,' said

67

Wriggly Worm.

The little Brown Snails stopped crying at once and pressed around Wriggly Worm even closer.

'What will you do, Wriggly? Are you going to fight him?'

'If I have to!' answered Wriggly Worm bravely, even though this Evil Weevil was probably very big and very fiercesome. 'In your playground did you say? Then I think I'll just go across and find out what that horrible Weevil is doing.'

To cries of 'Oooh, do be careful Wriggly!' off he went. In and out of the clumps of rough grass and through the fallen leaves under the horse chestnut trees, until he came to that special part where the Brown Snails had their playground.

There were twig slides and see-saws and a splendid tree-bark climbing frame, with leaf mats all around. There was no sign of Evil Weevil.

'Is there anyone there?' called Wriggly Worm. No answer.

Then, from underneath the leaf mats in front of the climbing frame came a crunching, chewing noise.

'Is that you, Evil Weevil?' called Wriggly Worm.

This time there was a nasty horrible laugh, but still no sign of Evil Weevil.

Wriggly Worm became rather cross.

'If you really are an Evil Weevil, why don't

you come out and show yourself?' he c

The leaf mats moved – just a little. Then, underneath the leaves came crawling a creatu so small it could hardly be seen at all.

'So you're Evil!' said Wriggly Worm.

He was astonished to find this creature was neither big nor fiercesome after all.

'Yes, I am,' said Evil Weevil, trying to sound important. '*And* I'm a cousin of the great Boring Woodbeetle, I am,' he said, although he had never actually met Boring.

'Well, what are you doing in the Brown Snails' playground?' demanded Wriggly Worm.

'Eating,' snapped Evil Weevil and began chewing the side of the climbing frame again. 'I don't know anything about playgrounds. But these are some of the most tasty pieces I've found for miles around.'

And he laughed his nasty, horrible laugh again.

'Stop it! Stop it at once,' yelled Wriggly Worm. 'If you keep on like that, there'll be nothing left of the little Brown Snails' playground.'

'But I'm hungry!' complained Evil Weevil. 'And I can't help it. I always laugh like that when I'm hungry. Perhaps you can tell me where else I can get a good feed.'

'Yes,' said Wriggly Worm, 'as a matter of fact, I can. Your cousin Boring's home is full of all

rare delights. That's where you should
. . . hy don't you pay him a visit?'

. . . vil Weevil didn't seem to be too certain
. . . bout this.

'Yes, well . . .' he giggled nervously, 'I am only
a very distant cousin. Boring is so much higher
up in the family tree. He may not welcome a
visit from a humble weevil like me.'

'Oh, nonsense,' declared Wriggly Worm, 'I
know Boring very well indeed and I'll arrange
for you to meet him.'

Evil Weevil was greatly impressed. He forgot
to chew. He forgot to laugh his horrible laugh.

'Would you? Could you?' was all he could
say.

'Yes, well,' said Wriggly Worm. 'First of all you
must mend the little Brown Snails' climbing
frame.'

'Oh sure!' replied Evil Weevil eagerly and set
to work. So in no time at all Wriggly Worm and
Evil Weevil were crawling across to Boring's
imposing residence. Then Wriggly Worm
shouted, 'Boring, there's someone here who's
dying to meet you.'

'Oh, jolly good show,' Boring called back, as
he came flying down at once from his lofty attic.
And 'Tophole chaps!' when Wriggly Worm had
introduced him to Evil Weevil.

Boring was delighted to meet a distant cousin.

He would be able to tell him all the th...
Boring family stories he knew if Evil V...
would come to stay with him.

'Look, I say, Evily Weevily old thing, you must come and stay with me for just as long as you like,' said Boring.

And Evil Weevil, who had never heard any of Boring's stories before, was delighted. So he stayed with Boring all through the long and dreary winter.

As for Wriggly Worm, he told the little Brown Snails, 'There's no Evil Weevil now in your playground. You can play there again whenever you like.'

They all said, 'Oh, thank you, Wriggly Worm, you are wonderful.'

And of course, he is, isn't he?

Dad's cough and the peculiar plant

Judith Drazin

Are you sitting comfortably? Then I'll begin.

'Where's our Dad gone?' said Joey.

'Where's our Dad gone?' said Lynne.

'Bother the man,' said Mum. 'He's got a cough and gone to bed.'

Dad lay in bed with a nasty cough.

'Drink up your medicine,' said Mum.

'Drink up your medicine,' said Lynne and Joey.

'It tastes of rotten eggs,' said Dad. 'Give it to the plant and make some tea.'

The plant grew in an eggcup on the window sill. Soon the medicine made it grow and grow.

72

Mum put the plant in her largest pudding basin. Dad lay in bed with a nasty cough.

'Drink up your medicine,' said Mum.

'Drink up your medicine,' said Lynne and Joey.

'It tastes of old boots,' said Dad. 'Give it to the plant and make some tea.'

The plant grew and grew until it reached the ceiling. Mum put the plant in her bright new saucepan. Dad lay in bed with a nasty cough.

'Drink up your medicine,' said Mum.

'Drink up your medicine,' said Lynne and Joey.

'It tastes of wet socks,' said Dad. 'Give it to the plant and make some tea.'

Still the plant grew and grew. Its shoots reached right across the room. They reached right to the bed and tickled Dad's nose. They wound round Mum's legs when she swept the floor.

'Bother that plant,' said Mum. 'Take it to the flower show to win a prize.'

Dad got slowly out of bed. He put the plant in a wheelbarrow and took it to the show.

'That plant has won a lot of money,' said the judge. 'That plant is the finest in the whole show.'

'Good old Dad,' said Lynne and Joey and Mum.

'Now I can have some ice-cream,' said Lynne.

'Now I can go to the football match,' said Joey.

'Now I can buy a new hat,' said Mum.

'Now my cough is quite better,' said Dad. 'And I can go home to have some tea.'

Thomas and the Monster

Marjorie Stannard

Are you sitting comfortably? Then I'll begin.

Thomas put on his wellies and his lucky woollen hat and walked up the garden path.

'I see you've got your lucky hat on,' remarked Snoodles the tortoise, who was just waking up from a nap on the grass. 'Are you going somewhere special?'

'Just looking for Monsters,' said Thomas. 'There might be one at the bottom, where the stream is.'

'Well, don't shout for me if you find one,' said Snoodles sleepily. 'I'm just going to have another little sleep in the rhubarb patch.'

75

Thomas walked on under the cherry trees until he came to the little summer-house by the stream. It was very quiet down here. The stream was half dried up and only made a soft murmur as it ran and the birds only twittered now and then because they were resting in green branches away from the hot sun.

He walked round the summer-house and looked in through its small dusty window. He couldn't see very well because the dust was quite thick, so he rubbed the glass with his lucky woollen hat.

Then he looked again. Inside was a wooden table with two chairs. On the table lay a heap of red cherries. And sitting on one of the chairs was a Monster.

Thomas knew he was a Monster because his hair was green and very short, like fur; and he had two horns sticking out – one above each ear.

Thomas put on his lucky hat again and opened the door.

'Hallo,' he said, 'are you a Monster?'

The Monster looked rather frightened. 'I hope you don't mind me being here,' he said nervously in a kind of choky voice, as though he had a sore throat. 'I couldn't find anywhere else to sleep. And I had a few cherries.'

Thomas sat down on the other chair. 'I don't mind at all,' he said. And he gave the Monster a handful of cherries and took some himself.

'I was on my way back to the mountains,' the Monster explained, putting his cherry-stones neatly in a row, 'when somehow I took a wrong turning. I got mixed up with motorways and railway stations and yards full of buses. Nobody saw me because I'm rather good at dodging underneath things. In the end I found myself in your garden. I am quite worn out. So I had a drink of stream-water and a few cherries, and came in here.'

'You can stay as long as you want,' said Thomas kindly. 'Which mountains are you going to?'

'This year,' said the Monster, 'I'm going to Wales. My uncle told me of a nice dry cave by a lake that will just suit me.'

'I think my Dad's got a map of England and Wales,' said Thomas, looking excited. 'Wait here for me.' And he ran up the path into the house. Thomas went into the kitchen and asked Mum if he could borrow the map for a little while. Mum got it out of the bureau drawer for him.

'Be careful with it,' said Mum, 'and put it back in the drawer when you've finished.'

Thomas carried the map down to the garden shed and spread it out on the table so that the Monster could see it properly. After a little while he said happily, 'Now I see where I went wrong!

Do you mind if I take a few cherries in my pocket? Thank you very much. I'll be on my way now. And if ever you come to that lake in North Wales I showed you, be sure to look me up. My relations will all be very pleased to meet you. I suppose,' he added, blinking his rather beautiful green eyes, 'I suppose you wouldn't let me try on your hat before I go?'

Thomas was a little doubtful if it would fit him, as he had a couple of horns to manage; but when Thomas passed it over he put it on his head quite easily, letting the horns poke through on each side.

'It *does* feel nice and warm,' said the Monster, giving a sort of sigh. And he was just going to take it off when Thomas said suddenly, 'No, you keep it. It's a lucky hat, so I'm sure you'll get to Wales all right.'

The Monster beamed. 'I'll be off, then. Good-bye!'

And he hurried through the door and disappeared among the bushes.

Thomas folded the map up carefully. Then he looked at the Monster's cherry-stones lying in a neat row.

'I'll keep them,' said Thomas to himself. 'Then nobody can say I haven't really seen a Monster.'

When he got back to the kitchen Mum said,

'Where's your lucky hat?'

'I've lent it to a Monster,' said Thomas.

'Well,' said Mum, 'it was time you had a new one, anyway.'

And that very evening she started to knit him a new one.

King Greenfingers and the giant rhubarb

Gordon Snell

Are you sitting comfortably? Then I'll begin.

King Greenfingers was very proud of all the fruit and vegetables which grew in his palace garden. He loved to walk about, gazing at the peas and beans and lettuces and apples and plums. It was much nicer than the garden of the King next door, who only grew strawberries and nothing else.

But King Greenfingers was worried about the rhubarb: it just wouldn't grow. So one day he asked a magician to put a spell on it so that it would grow into the tallest rhubarb in the world.

The magician danced around the rhubarb patch, chanting and sprinkling a magic potion from his watering-can.

'Abra Fabra Labra Lo,
This will make your rhubarb grow
Not too fast and not too slow
Abra Fabra Labra Lo.'

Next day, King Greenfingers hurried out into his garden. Yes, the rhubarb was definitely a little bit taller. The next day it came up to his knees; the next, it reached his waist; and soon it was as tall as the King himself.

'Look,' he called over the wall to the King next door, who was picking strawberries as usual, 'my rhubarb is as tall as I am.'

'So it is,' said the King next door. 'Have a strawberry.'

The rhubarb grew and grew until it was as tall as a giraffe.

'Look,' called King Greenfingers, 'my rhubarb is as tall as a giraffe.'

'So it is,' said the King next door. 'Have a strawberry.'

The rhubarb grew until it was as tall as a double-decker bus. Then it grew as tall as a palm tree. Then it grew as tall as Nelson's Column in Trafalgar Square.

'Look,' said King Greenfingers, 'my rhubarb is as tall as Nelson's Column.'

'So it is,' said the King next door. 'Have a strawberry.'

The rhubarb patch spread so that it was like a great forest, and the stalks were like thick tree-trunks. One day, King Greenfingers got a huge ladder and climbed up and up until he was among the green leafy bits at the top of the rhubarb stalks. He poked his head out and saw the King next door, far away below in his garden, picking strawberries.

'Look,' he called, 'my rhubarb is the tallest rhubarb in the world!'

'So it is,' the King next door called back. 'But what does it taste like?'

'Taste like?' said King Greenfingers. 'Well, I don't . . . I mean I haven't . . . that is . . . I'm sure it's the tastiest rhubarb in the world, too.'

Then he climbed down and gave orders to his cooks to cut down some of the rhubarb. They came out with axes and saws, and chopped down a lot of the stalks which crashed to the ground with a great noise like falling trees. Then they sawed the stalks into pieces and made them into a giant pie.

King Greenfingers took one piece and handed another piece over the garden wall to the King next door. They each took a bite. Then they chewed and chewed and chewed and chewed, and finally swallowed. They both looked a bit pale and rubbed their stomachs as though they had a pain. Then King Greenfingers gave a faint smile.

'Well, how do you like it?' he asked.

The King next door thought it tasted really awful but he didn't like to say so. And King Greenfingers thought it tasted really awful but he didn't like to say so either – especially after all his boasting. Neither of them could face the idea of having another bite. Then the King next door had an idea.

'That rhubarb,' he said, 'has such an amazing taste, it is too good to eat. I think you should keep it in a museum, so that people can come and marvel at the pie made from the tallest rhubarb in the world.'

'What a good idea!' said King Greenfingers with a sigh of relief.

So now, while people come to stare at the giant pie in its refrigerated glass case in the Rhubarb Pie Museum, the two Kings spend many pleasant hours together. Sometimes, King Greenfingers climbs over the wall to eat strawberries with the King next door. And sometimes the King next door comes over to *his* garden, and they go for a picnic in the rhubarb forest. They like to sit in the shade of the rhubarb – but neither of them ever suggests trying to eat it.

The pale purple pullover

Emma Milton

Are you sitting comfortably? Then I'll begin.

The night before the school fair, Auntie Kay came to stay. She brought Benjie a present. It was a pale purple pullover. Benjie put it on. 'Lovely!' said Auntie Kay. 'Lovely!' said Mummy. 'Lovely!' said Daddy.

Benjie went through to his bedroom. He looked in the mirror – 'Yak!' he said. (He didn't think it looked lovely.)

After tea Mummy said, 'Will you post my letter for me, Benjie?'

Auntie Kay said, 'And will you wear your pale purple pullover?'

Benjie looked out of the window. It was nearly dark. 'Yes,' he said, 'I will.' There were lights in all the houses. It was almost too dark to see. Nobody saw Benjie's pale purple pullover at all.

Next morning Benjie took his dog, Tweed, for a walk. It was especially early because of the school fair.

Auntie Kay said, 'Will you wear your pale purple pullover?'

Benjie looked out the window. The birds were just waking up. 'Yes,' he said, 'I will.'

The hills were edged with gold. The sun was just getting up. Nobody saw Benjie's pale purple pullover at all. After breakfast everyone got ready to go to the school fair.

Auntie Kay said, 'Will you wear your pale purple pullover?' Benjie looked out the window. The sun was shining brightly. 'Not today,' said Benjie, 'It's too warm. I'll wear my grey shirt and my grey trousers.' Benjie liked the school fair.

He carried around toffee apples on a wooden tray. Everybody bought one. Benjie bought the last one himself and sat in the sun and ate it.

Benjie liked the pony rides. He had three rides on a little grey pony called 'Trainer'. He gave Trainer the core of his toffee apple. Benjie liked the Silver Band.

RUMP TUMPTY TUM! RUMP TUMPTY TUM!

Benjie marched behind the band with all the other boys.

Daddy and Mummy and Auntie Kay sat in the sun with their jackets off. A cold wind sprang up. Auntie Kay put on her jacket. Mummy put on her jacket. Daddy put on his jacket. Auntie Kay took something out of her bag. She went over to the tent where Benjie was selling old clothes. 'It's getting cold,' Auntie Kay said, 'Here is your pale purple pullover.'

'Thank you, Auntie Kay,' Benjie said politely, and he hung the pullover over the back of the seat.

When it was time to go home, Benjie couldn't find his pale purple pullover. 'I'm afraid it's been sold by mistake!' said the big girl in charge, and she went to tell the teacher. 'I'm afraid it's been sold by mistake!' said the teacher, and he went to tell the Headmaster. 'I'm afraid it's been sold by mistake!' said the Headmaster and he looked very sad.

'Don't cry, Benjie!' said the big girl. 'Don't cry, Benjie!' said the teacher. 'Don't cry, Benjie!' said the Headmaster. 'Here's money to buy a new pullover!'

Then Daddy and Mummy and Auntie Kay went with Benjie to the shop that sold pullovers. They looked at pale blue pullovers, pale grey pullovers and even pale purple pullovers. Benjie

86

chose a pale grey pullover to match his shirt and shorts and he whistled all the way home.

Archie the singing donkey

Ann Burnett

Are you sitting comfortably? Then I'll begin.

Archie was a seaside donkey. Every summer he carried children up and down the sands.

'10p a ride! 10p a ride!' the donkey man would shout and the children would come running. Sometimes grown-ups would want a ride too, and once Archie had to carry a big fat man.

'My goodness,' he panted as he reached the end of the ride. 'I'm glad I don't have to do that every day.'

Archie was very fond of the children, especially if they gave him a lick of their ice-cream. It was just what he fancied on a hot day. His long tongue would come out and he'd slurp up the ice-cream.

'Delicious!' he'd breathe and look round to see if there was any more.

Now going up and down the same stretch of sand every day got a bit boring at times, so to amuse himself Archie would make up little songs like:

Hee Haw Twiddle Dee Dee
I'm a little Donkey
By the Sea.

or:

Clip Clop Off I Trot,
Oh My! Isn't it Hot!

But his favourite was:

Oh I do like a slurp of Ice-Cream
Oh I do like a bite of Choc Ice Bar,
Oh I do like an Ice-Cream in my Tum, Tum, Tum
Tiddly um tum tum
Tiddly um tum tum.

He'd hum his little songs to himself as he plodded up and down, and sometimes he'd like them so much he'd give a loud Hee Haw!

'Just listen to Archie,' the children would say. 'He's enjoying himself.'

One day, things were very quiet. Only a few children wanted a donkey ride.

'It's this singing competition along at the pier,' said the donkey man. 'Everyone's gone there to watch it.'

And he sat down on the sand to rest till everybody came back again.

'Oh, well, hee haw,' yawned Archie, 'I might as well go along for a look at it.'

And off he set.

When he got there, a man was standing on the stage singing a song about pirates.

'Yo, ho, ho,' he sang, 'and a bottle of rum!'

But the audience didn't like him and booed.

Then a tall lady got up but nobody could make out the words she was singing so everybody started booing again.

Suddenly Archie found himself getting up on the stage and bowing to the audience.

'Why, it's Archie,' the audience whispered. 'Can he sing?'

Archie immediately launched into:

Oh I do like a slurp of an Ice-Cream
Oh I do like a bite of Choc Ice Bar,
Oh I do like an Ice-Cream in my Tum, Tum, Tum,
Tiddly um tum tum
Tiddly um tum tum.

The audience cheered loudly for an encore, so he sang:

Hee Haw Twiddle Dee Dee

I'm a little Donkey
By the Sea,

and:

Clip Clop Off I Trot
Oh My! Isn't it Hot!

The audience cheered even louder.

'Hurray for Archie!' they shouted.

The compere held up his hands for silence. 'Ladies and gentlemen,' he announced. 'The winner of our singing competition is ... ARCHIE!'

'Hurray!' yelled everyone.

The man held up his hands again. 'And the prize is ... an ice-cream every day for a month!'

'Hee Haw!' brayed Archie. 'Oh my, just what I wished for. Hee Haw!'

'Hurray!' cheered the crowd. 'Hurray for Archie the singing donkey!'

'Hee Haw, Hee Haw, Hee Haw,' sang Archie happily.

Lazy Witch to the rescue

Eleanor Tims

Are you sitting comfortably? Then I'll begin.

'I'm bored,' said Lazy Witch.

'Me too,' said Smudge, her cat.

'Let's go for a ride,' she suggested. She called her broomstick, which was leaning in the corner, looking bored and covered with dust.

'And I'm bored with this old broomstick, too,' she said. So she changed it into a huge, shining, Rolls Royce car. Then she changed her mind and turned it into a rocket.

'That's better,' they both said, and climbed on board.

'I'll do the count-down,' said Smudge, and

92

'I'll be the pilot,' said Lazy Witch.

10 9 8 7 6 5 4 3 2 1 ZERO! SWOOSH. They zoomed into the sky. Clouds floated past them; the birds they met looked a bit surprised.

'This is a nice change from being at home,' said Lazy Witch.

'*Danger, danger*!' yelled Smudge. 'Look below.'

They were passing over a country covered in ice.

A great big polar bear was chasing a little Eskimo boy. Quickly Lazy Witch zoomed down.

'Jump on,' they shouted to the little Eskimo boy.

'Thank you,' he said politely. 'That bear wanted to eat me.'

Lazy Witch took him home to his igloo. His parents were very glad to see him.

10 9 8 7 6 5 4 3 2 1 ZERO! counted Smudge. SWOOSH. They zoomed off up into the sky.

'*Danger, danger*!' yelled Smudge. 'Look below.'

They were passing over a forest. A kangaroo was leaping this way and that, trying to escape from a terrible forest fire.

Quickly Lazy Witch zoomed down.

The kangaroo jumped on. She had a baby in her pouch.

'Thank you,' she said gratefully. 'The fire was going to burn us up.'

Lazy Witch took her to another part of the

country, well away from the danger of fire.

10 9 8 7 6 5 4 3 2 1 ZERO! counted Smudge. They zoomed off up into the sky.

'*Danger, danger*!' yelled Smudge. 'Look below.'

They were passing over some fields where there were men with guns. In front of them, a little rabbit was running. Quickly, Lazy Witch zoomed down and the rabbit jumped aboard.

'Thank you,' he said, puffing. 'Those men were thinking of making me into rabbit stew.'

Lazy Witch took him to stay with some friends.

10 9 8 7 6 5 4 3 2 1 ZERO! They zoomed off up into the sky.

'*Danger, danger*!' yelled Smudge. 'Look below.'

They were passing above the seaside. The beach was full of people, but none of them had noticed a little girl, floating out to sea on a rubber mattress. Quickly, Lazy Witch zoomed down and the little girl jumped on.

'Thank you,' she gasped. 'The waves were carrying me away.'

Lazy Witch took her back to her parents on the beach. They had thought she was playing further along, and hadn't even missed her.

Then Lazy Witch started to zoom back. But something was wrong.

'I didn't do the count-down,' said Smudge, and he counted: 10 9 8 7 6 5 4 3 2 1 ZERO!

Splutter. Splutter. Cough. Cough, went the engine.

It didn't like sea-water and it didn't like sand.

'Oh dear,' said Lazy Witch. 'I never bothered to learn the spell to get us out of a breakdown.'

'This isn't much fun,' said the rocket, and he changed himself back into a broomstick.

'That's the trouble, living with Lazy Witch,' he went on. 'If you want anything doing, you have to do it yourself.'

They lifted off and in a moment were back home.

'All the same,' said Smudge, 'We've done a lot of things today.'

'Yes, and I'm tired,' yawned Lazy Witch, curling up on her bed.

'So am I,' purred Smudge, and he curled up beside her. In a moment they were both asleep and the broomstick leaned in his corner and snoozed, too.

MORE STORIES FROM
LISTEN WITH MOTHER

MORE STORIES FROM

LISTEN
WITH MOTHER

Illustrated by Priscilla Lamont

Contents

Preface   9
  Nerys Hughes
The night dad brought home a pig   11
  Judith Drazin
Fishfingers and custard   14
  Jane Holiday
The flying rabbit   18
  Kenneth McLeish
The crotchety tooth   24
  Margaret Hopkins
The Hippo who tried to catch cold   29
  Daphne Lister
The guineapig show   33
  Armorel Kay Walling
Susie's hair ribbon   36
  Malcolm Carrick
Constantinople   39
  Peter Ashley and Janey Gordon
Constantinople goes shopping   44
  Peter Ashley and Janey Gordon

Clever old foxy   49
    Eugenie Summerfield
The dog who had no name   53
    Leila Berg
Fingy and the garden   57
    Diana Webb
Fingy and the magic stone   61
    Diana Webb
A hat for Bethan   65
    Gill Davies
'Fraidy mouse   68
    Anne Wellington
The ballad of Bad Belinda   72
    Moira Miller
The giant brothers and the army   78
    Val Annan
Young hedgehog helps rabbit   82
    Vera Rushbrooke
Teddy bear gets too fat for his jacket   86
    Margaret Gore
Alison's new baby   92
    Shelley R. Lee
The treat   96
    Edna Williams
Smarticat   99
    Anne Wellington
The lippity loppity rabbit with the
    empty basket   104
    Judith Drazin

Gilbert the ostrich   107
  Jane Holiday
The dragon of Penhesgyn   110
  Moira Miller
Angela and the custard pump   116
  Jan Dean
Amy Kate's lion   120
  Joyce Williams
All it needs is a wash   125
  Armorel Kay Walling

Preface

I've always liked telling stories. When I was at boarding-school I used to frighten the wits out of the girls in the 'dorm', telling gruesome ghost stories when the lights were out!

I love reading stories on the radio – for grown-ups and children. But best of all, I like reading to my own children. Ben is seven now and can read for himself but he still loves snuggling up and being read to. (He would die if he knew I'd told you that.) Mari-Claire is two and a half and a live Jumping Bean from about 6 a.m. to 7 p.m., when she reluctantly agrees to leave the action and go to bed. But for about ten minutes she will sit *completely* still if I read to her.

What I mean is, reading stories is so much more than the act of speaking out loud the printed page; it's an involvement with each other as a little unit – parent and child – a shared and imaginative experience. This is why 'Listen with Mother' is such a comforting *timeless* phrase and why the programme is so durable. I listened to it with my Mum, and Mari-Claire listens to it with me.

And I love taking part in it – it's a joy!

Some of the best stories are in this book. So, for the Jumping Bean and thousands of children everywhere, are you sitting comfortably? Then I'll begin.

Nerys Hughes

The night Dad brought home a pig

Judith Drazin

Are you sitting comfortably? Then I'll begin.

'Where's our Dad gone?' said Joey.

'Where's our Dad gone?' said Lynne.

'Bother the man,' said Mum, 'he's gone to the fair to win a pig.'

That night Dad came home with a pink pig under one arm.

'Bother the man,' said Mum, 'where can we put a pig in a high-up flat?'

The pig spent the night in the downstairs laundry. He tramped over Grandpa's clean shirts and he tried to eat Mum's best blue pillow case.

'Bother the pig,' said Mum, 'take it away and bring back something else.'

'All right, all right, all right,' said Dad, 'I will go out and do a swop.'

'I wonder what Dad will bring,' said Joey.

'I wonder what Dad will bring,' said Lynne.

That night Dad came home with a statue. It was a lady with a long dress and long hair.

'Bother the man,' said Mum, 'where can a statue go without a garden?'

In the end they put the statue on the balcony. She got all tangled up with Mum's washing line.

'All right, all right, all right,' said Dad, 'I will go out and do a swop.'

'What will he bring home next?' said Joey.

'What will he bring home next?' said Lynne.

That night there was a terrible noise on the stairs. Dad was bringing home a piano with his friend from along the street.

'Now we can all have a bit of music,' said Dad.

'Bother the man,' said Mum, 'that piano is much too big to get through the door.'

The piano spent the night on the landing. Grandpa bumped into it on his way upstairs and was very cross.

'All right, all right, all right,' said Dad, 'I am just going out to do a swop.'

Dad went out for a long, long time. That night he came home with nothing under his arm.

'Why didn't you bring anything?' said Joey.

'Why didn't you bring anything?' said Lynne.

Dad gave a big smile. 'How would you like to go on a trip?' he said. 'How would you like to go on a trip to the seaside?'

'Can I have ice-cream?' said Joey.

'Can I go paddling all day long?' said Lynne.

'Can I sit in a deckchair and put my feet up?' said Mum.

'That's right,' said Dad, 'I swopped the pig for a statue and I swopped the statue for a piano and I swopped the piano for a trip to the seaside. Now Lynne can go paddling and Joey can eat ice-cream and Mum can sit in a deckchair with her feet up.'

'Good old Dad,' said Joey.

'Good old Dad,' said Lynne.

'Why, bless the man,' said Mum, 'it's just what I wanted.'

And off she went to make a cup of tea.

Fishfingers and custard

Jane Holiday

Are you sitting comfortably? Then I'll begin.

'What do you want for your dinner, love?' Sharon's Mum asked her.

'I'm just having an apple and a banana but *you* must have something cooked.'

'Mm . . . .' Sharon thought for a moment. 'Fishfingers please,' she said at last, 'and . . . custard.'

'*Fishfingers* and *custard*?' said her Mum. 'Fishfingers and custard? You can't have that.'

'Why not?' Sharon asked grumpily. 'Why can't I? You asked me! You asked me what I wanted.'

'You can't have it,' said her mother, 'because you *don't* eat fishfingers with custard. You can have fishfingers and chips though, and some nice green peas.'

Sharon was cross.

She covered all the fishfingers and all the chips and all the peas with tomato ketchup.

Then she cut it all up into teeny tiny pieces.

Then she put salt and pepper on it.

Then she ate it – as *slowly* as she possibly could.

Sharon's Mum sighed. 'Do eat up Sharon,' she said. 'It'll get cold.'

'Don't care,' said Sharon, but she ate it up at last because she *was* hungry.

Next day Sharon's Dad cooked her dinner.

'What do you want for dinner, Sharon?' asked Dad. 'I'm just having a cheese sandwich but you ought to have something cooked.'

'Fishfingers and custard please,' said Sharon, quick as a flash.

'No you don't!' laughed Dad. 'You had fishfingers yesterday, didn't you? I'll cook you some sausage and mash.'

Sharon was cross.

She covered all the sausages and all the mashed potato with tomato ketchup. Then she cut it all up into teeny tiny pieces.

Sharon's Dad sighed.

'Eat up Sharon,' he said. 'I cook a lovely meal and you just mess it about.'

Sharon scowled, but she ate it up at last because she was hungry.

The next day Sharon went to see Granny and had dinner with her.

'Now what would you like for dinner, Sharon?' Gran asked her. 'I'm having a boiled egg because I don't eat much.'

'Can I have whatever I like?' asked Sharon.

'Yes,' said Granny, 'as long as I've got it in the house.'

'Then I want *fishfingers* and *custard*,' said Sharon. 'That's what I want, please, Granny.'

'Right,' said Granny. 'Pass my little milk-saucepan dear, will you?'

In a few minutes they sat down to eat.

In front of Granny was a lovely brown egg in an eggcup, with bread and butter on a plate beside it.

In Sharon's place was a plate with three fishfingers on it. Next to it on a little mat stood a small jug.

'Help yourself to custard dear,' Granny said calmly, tapping her egg with a spoon.

Sharon poured the thick yellow custard over her fishfingers. 'At last,' she thought.

'What did you have for dinner?' Mum and Dad asked her that evening when she was back home.

'Fishfingers and custard,' said Sharon.

'Oh!' said Mum, sounding a bit cross.

'Oh!' said Dad. He didn't sound very pleased either.

'It was *horrible*,' said Sharon. 'But I ate it all up because Granny made it *specially*.'

'You little fusspot!' laughed Dad. 'You keep on asking for fishfingers and custard and when you

16

get it, you don't like it!'

'You're a big silly,' said Mum.

'So what do you want to eat for dinner tomorrow then?' asked Dad.

'I know *just* what I want!' said Sharon. 'Something *really* nice!'

'What?' asked Mum and Dad.

'SAUSAGES and RASPBERRY JAM,' said Sharon.

'Oh . . . Sharon!' said her Mum. 'You're *impossible*!'

The flying rabbit

Kenneth McLeish

Are you sitting comfortably? Then I'll begin.

One day, Small Rabbit was out in the meadow, as usual. He looked up at the birds in the sky. He thought to himself, 'I'm tired of walking about on the ground all the time. I'm going to fly, like the birds.'

He climbed a tree. It wasn't easy, because his front legs were too short and his back legs were too long.

When he was half way up, he looked down. The ground was a long way off. 'All right,' he thought. 'Now's the time to fly!'

He spread his front legs out like wings, and gave a great big rabbit-jump off his branch.

But he was lucky, for just underneath his flying-branch was the nest of the Crow family. He landed in it with a bump.

'Ow!' said the two little crows. 'Watch where you're falling!'

Small Rabbit didn't answer. He was wondering why he hadn't been able to fly. 'Can you fly?' he asked the little crows.

'Not yet,' they answered. 'But we will one day, if we try hard enough.'

'So will I,' said Small Rabbit. 'I'll stay here with you until then.'

Small Rabbit stayed in the Crows' nest all day. It was a bit of a squeeze, especially when Mr and Mrs Crow came back. They weren't pleased to find a new rabbit baby in their nest.

As it began to get dark, Mrs Rabbit noticed that Small was missing. She went out to the edge of the field to look for him. 'Small?' she called. 'Sma-all! Where are you?'

'Up here,' said Small, poking his head over the side of the Crows' nest.

'Good gracious! Whatever are you doing up there?' asked Mrs Rabbit.

'Learning to fly.'

'Come down, you silly child. Rabbits don't fly.'

'I won't come down.'

His mother went back to the burrow and fetched Mr Rabbit. He came and sat beside her under the tree. 'Be careful, Small,' he said. 'It's a long way down.'

All the nine little rabbits came too. They all sat in a row under the tree, looking up at Small.

No one knew what to do. Mr and Mrs Crow began to get cross. 'Look,' they said to Small. 'you can't stay here all night. There isn't room.'

'It won't take all night,' answered Small. 'As soon as I can fly, I'll go.'

'But rabbits can't fly,' shouted the Crows.

'In that case, I'll make rabbit history,' answered Small.

The Crows got angrier and angrier. The two baby crows were squashed under Small's furry tail. The big crows had to sit hanging over the edge of the nest. They looked like umbrellas that hadn't been folded up properly.

At last Mr Crow lost his temper. 'You stay here,' he said to Mrs Crow. 'I'm going out.' And off he flew.

So there they all sat, eleven rabbits in the field under the tree, and one rabbit and three crows in the nest. The biggest crow was hanging over the edge. The shadows of night began to creep across the field.

Mr Crow was away a long time. At last, just as the sun was beginning to disappear behind the hills, he came flying back. He landed on the side of the nest, and nearly fell off again, there was so little room.

'It's all right,' he said. 'I've been to see Owl and he's told me what to do.'

'What did he say?' asked Mrs Crow.

'Come up here and I'll tell you,' answered Mr Crow.

Mr and Mrs Crow flew to a branch higher up the tree, and he whispered into her ear behind his wing. No one else said anything. The eleven rabbits in the field, and the one rabbit and two crows in the nest, sat still and waited.

At last Mr and Mrs Crow came back. 'Come on, little crows,' said Mr Crow. 'Time to be going.'

'Going? Going where?' said the little crows.

'To the rabbit warren, of course. If rabbits are going to start flying, crows will have to start living in holes in the ground. Down we go!'

He picked up one of the little crows in his beak, and flew off. Mrs Crow elbowed Small out of the way with her wing, and flew off with the other little crow. They circled round and down, towards the rabbit burrow on the other side of the field.

Small watched them go. All at once he began to feel lonely. The sun had almost gone. He was getting cold, all on his own in the nest. He looked down. The eleven rabbits from his family were still sitting on the ground watching him.

'I . . . I think I'd better come down,' he said.

'All right,' said Mr Rabbit. 'Are you going to fly?'

'Not today. I don't feel much like flying any more. Rabbits ought to stay on the ground, and leave flying to the birds.'

'How will you get down then?'

'I'll have to jump,' said Small nervously. 'Will you catch me?'

'You can't jump,' his mother said. 'You'll hurt yourself.'

'I know,' said Mr Rabbit suddenly. He whispered to the other rabbits. Then he and Mrs Rabbit lay down, and Large climbed on to their backs. When he was ready the Medium Twins climbed up and balanced on top of his head. Then the bravest of the Triplets climbed up and stood on their heads. Soon there was a ladder of rabbits, reaching all the way up to the Crows' nest. The baby rabbits were too small to climb, but they stood by ready to catch anyone who fell.

'Come on, Small,' said Mr Rabbit in a squashed sort of voice. 'Be quick, before we all fall over.'

As soon as Small was down, the rabbit ladder unsorted itself.

'Thank goodness for that,' said Mr Rabbit. 'It was flat work being at the bottom.'

'Don't ever do a thing like that again,' said Mrs Rabbit crossly to Small. 'Look what's happened now. We've got a family of Crows moved into our burrow. How are we going to get rid of them?'

But there was no need. As soon as the Crow family saw that their nest was empty, they flew back and put the baby crows safely inside it. 'We'll move into a new one tomorrow. As high as we can go,' said Mr Crow.

That's why, if you go and look, you'll find that all crows live in nests right at the top of very high trees. And rabbits stay on the ground.

The crotchety tooth

Margaret Hopkins

Are you sitting comfortably? Then I'll begin.

Once there were two rows of happy little teeth. One row was up at the top of the mouth, the other row was down at the bottom, and they worked together every mealtime chewing meat and peas and sausages and apple tart. Sometimes there was jelly, which was easy because they didn't have to bite that. Sometimes there were crisps, and they did enjoy making a crunchy crackly sound as they munched away at them. And sometimes there were sweets, and then they could crunch them up quickly if they liked, or, if they felt tired, they could leave them alone and make them last a long time.

So all day long the teeth were kept busy. The little sharp ones at the front would bite off the food, and the wide knobbly ones at the back would chew it up into small pieces. And at night the upper row cuddled down next to the lower one, and they all went quietly to sleep.

Then one morning at breakfast something strange happened. The little teeth were busy with a boiled egg and bread and butter fingers, when one of the bottom front teeth said, 'Ow! That piece of crust hurt!'

'Don't be silly,' said his twin brother next to him, 'crusts can't hurt.'

'Well that one did,' said the first tooth crossly. 'Ow! So did that. I'm not going to bite anything more this breakfast time. Let the teeth round the corner do it all.'

So for the rest of that meal the food had to come in sideways so that the other teeth could bite it.

Then again at dinner time the crotchety tooth said, 'Ow! That piece of potato hurt!'

'Don't be silly,' said his twin again, 'potatoes can't hurt.'

'That one did,' said the crotchety tooth, and once again he refused to bite anything more.

This went on for two days. Then one evening when they were settling down to sleep, one of the top teeth, the one who liked to cuddle up against the crotchety tooth, suddenly said to him, 'Keep still, can't you? You're wiggling around and keeping me awake.'

'I want to wiggle,' said the crotchety tooth. 'I want to wiggle and wiggle.'

'Don't be silly,' said his twin sleepily, 'teeth

can't wiggle.'

'But I can!' the crotchety tooth cried out. 'Just feel me then!' And he moved backwards and forwards so much that the teeth on either side of him could feel that he certainly was loose.

'Stop it,' said his friend from above. 'How can we sleep with you doing that?'

'I don't care!' he giggled. 'I'm clever! I can do what you can't do. I can wiggle like this, and this. Ow! It hurt that time. All right, I won't move any more tonight.'

He went to sleep soon after that, tired out by all his wiggling. But the other teeth stayed awake for a long time, whispering about him.

'I can't understand it,' said the one from the top row. 'Teeth don't move. Teeth can't move. But he did. It's very strange.'

And it grew stranger. After two more days even the teeth right at the very back could see that the crotchety tooth could wiggle so much that sometimes he seemed to be lying right down.

And he did no work at all. He wouldn't let food come anywhere near him. This meant that the teeth near him couldn't do anything either, and the back teeth were getting tired out with all the extra work they had to do.

Then came the strangest thing of all.

It was evening, and the teeth had had their scrub and were ready for bed when some of the front teeth saw that there was an apple coming. Now they were bored with doing nothing all day, so before the crotchety tooth could say 'no' they took a big bite.

'*Owwww*!' screamed the crotchety tooth. 'That's not fair! I didn't want to bite! And I won't bite ever again! I'm going to jump out and leave you all.'

With that he hopped out of his place and never came back again. What happened to him then? The other teeth never knew for sure. They did see him being put under the pillow, but next morning when the pillow was lifted up they saw that he had gone, quite gone. There was some shiny money there, but no tooth.

They had to start breakfast with one biter missing. This wasn't too bad, they found, in fact it was easier than it had been the day before, because at least the rest of the front teeth were allowed to do their proper work. But they found it hard to bite together properly and this worried them.

'How can we manage with a big gap like this?' asked one of them. 'We need a tooth in that space.'

'Please, Sir,' squeaked a little voice, 'please, Sir. I'm growing as quickly as I can.'

'Who said that?' asked another one.

'Please sir,' came the squeaky voice again,

'please, I'm the new tooth. I'm growing in the gap.'

The teeth looked down into the gap and there, sure enough, was the tiny white tip of a new tooth coming up.

'How did you get there?' gasped all the teeth.

'I grew!' said the little one proudly. 'I've been growing for several days. I was trying to push that old tooth out. He was sitting on my head!'

'You poor dear thing,' said the others kindly.

'Well, you're as bad,' the new one replied indignantly. 'Some of you are sitting on top of my baby brothers. They're going to start pushing you out soon. You just wait and see. You'll be put under the pillow too.'

The other teeth all cried, 'Nonsense!' They thought that the new tooth was making it all up. He seemed too sweet to want to push them out. But the crotchety tooth's twin had been lonely since his brother had left, and he thought to himself, 'I think the new tooth is right. I think his brothers will push us out, but I don't mind leaving. I want to find my twin. I'd like to see what happens under the pillow and how the money gets there. I hope it will be my turn soon. Now I come to think of it, that crust at breakfast did hurt a bit.'

And so he looked forward to the time when he too would be loose enough to come out and go under the pillow.

The hippo who tried to catch cold

Daphne Lister

Are you sitting comfortably? Then I'll begin.

Once there was a small hippopotamus who wanted a handkerchief. He wanted one more than anything else in the world.

He asked his mother for one, but she said, 'Don't be silly! You haven't got a cold.'

Little Hippo thought about this for a while.

'Well,' he said to himself, 'I had better try and catch a cold and then maybe I can have a handkerchief.'

But he didn't know how to catch a cold, so he went to the park to think about it and lay down on the grass and soon he fell fast asleep. When he woke up some people were standing staring at him.

'I shouldn't lie there if I were you,' said an old lady kindly. 'The grass is damp and you might catch cold.'

'Goody!' said Little Hippo.

'What's good about catching cold?' said Tom the Postman, scratching his head.

'Well, then I can have a handkerchief,' explained Little Hippo.

Some children laughed. 'You don't need a cold to have a handkerchief,' said a little boy called Michael.

'*I* do,' said Little Hippo sadly. 'My mother can't think of any other reason to have one. Can you?'

'You *might* need one to collect conkers in,' suggested Michael, and he took a green handkerchief out of his pocket and held the corners together so that it made a little bag.

'Or to make a sunhat on a very hot day,' said Tom the Postman, taking out a big checked handkerchief and knotting the corners. Then he took off his postman's cap and put on the handkerchief sunhat.

'Or to bandage your foot if you had an accident,' said Sue the Nurse, and she folded her very clean white handkerchief to make a bandage.

'Or to dry your eyes if you hear a sad story and it makes you cry a little bit,' said the old lady, taking out a lavender coloured hanky with a lace edge, and dabbing her eyes.

'Or to find out which way the wind is blowing,' said Jack the Sailor, and he took out a large blue handkerchief and held it up in the air. 'Sou'-westerly, today,' he said.

'Or to make a toy rabbit,' said Michael's sister Ann, and she folded her little pink handkerchief round her fingers into the shape of a rabbit.

'Or to make a flag to fly if the Queen or anyone important comes,' said Michael's friend, Billy, taking out an orange handkerchief and knotting two corners to a stick.

Little Hippo smiled. 'So a handkerchief really *would* be very useful even if I *didn't* catch a cold?' he said.

'Yes,' everyone agreed. Then Ann said, 'Here, you can have mine,' and she gave Little Hippo the pink rabbit handkerchief.

'And mine,' said Michael, handing him the green hanky.

'And mine,' said Tom the Postman, taking the knotted hanky off his head.

One by one they all gave Little Hippo their handkerchiefs.

'Ooh, *thank* you,' said Little Hippo, and he was so pleased he turned head over heels on the

31

grass. Then he ran home to show them all to his mother.

'Mother!' he called, 'Look at – at – at – ATISHOO!'

And Little Hippo sneezed loudly.

'Dear me,' his mother said. 'You've caught a cold! How lucky that I've just been to buy you a handkerchief,' and she gave Little Hippo a huge brown hanky and he sneezed into it three times: ATCHOO! ATCHOO! ATCHOO!

'I'll keep this one for colds,' said Little Hippo snuffily, 'and the others for other things. You know, mother, handkerchiefs can be *such* useful things . . . a – a – ATISHOOO!'

The guineapig show

Armorel Kay Walling

Are you sitting comfortably? Then I'll begin.

Daddy said, 'There's a Guineapig Show on the Common.'

'A show?' cried Rachel. 'Singing and dancing? Oh *please* can we go?'

'Guineapigs singing and dancing?' laughed Daddy. 'No, not *that* kind of show! It's a competition – to find the most beautiful guineapig and give it a prize.'

'What prize?'

'A big blue ribbon, I expect,' said Daddy.

Rachel thought. 'I have the most beautiful guineapig in the world,' she said. 'Can we put *her* in the show?'

'Why not?' said Daddy.

So Rachel fetched Sunset, her guineapig. Sunset didn't *look* like the most beautiful guineapig in the world just then. She'd been playing in the muddy grass.

'We must do her hair,' said Daddy.

He shook some special guineapig shampoo into a bowl of warm water. Sunset didn't like having her hair washed. She went 'weeeeeeeek!' She looked sort of *flat*, too. Rachel felt sorry for her. She gave her a carrot to cheer her up, and let her dry by the warm stove. Then she fetched her dolly's brush. She brushed Sunset until she shone. Sunset liked that. She closed her eyes and s-t-r-e-t-c-h-e-d. And then, when Daddy had filed all her toenails, she *did* look beautiful.

'But don't cry if she *doesn't* win the prize,' said Daddy.

There was a big tent on the Common. Inside the tent were lots of tables. And on the tables were lots of cages. And in the cages were lots of guineapigs: lots and lots – more than Rachel thought lived in the whole world; big ones, little ones, smooth ones, fluffy ones, black ones, white ones, some all different colours like Sunset, and some with so much fur you couldn't tell which end was which!

There were lots of people, too.

A lady asked Rachel how old Sunset was, and wrote her name in a book. She stuck a number on Sunset's ear, and put her in a cage. Then a man in a white coat came to look. He looked at every guineapig – at their fur, and ears, and toenails, and teeth.

He put them back in their cages, and thought.

Then he picked up a big blue ribbon. He walked over to where Rachel and her Daddy were standing. He went up to Sunset's cage and then . . . he pinned the ribbon *on the cage next door*.

'Don't cry, Daddy,' said Rachel quickly. 'I'll find another blue ribbon to put on Sunset's cage tomorrow. After all, *we* know she's still the most beautiful guineapig in the world, don't we?'

'We do!' said Daddy, and felt happy again. He let Rachel go on the swings on the way home, so *she* felt happy too.

But Sunset felt *very* happy. Because for tea Rachel gave her some oats, *and* apple *and* carrot *and* a dandelion – which, if you're a guineapig, is even better than winning the prize in a Guineapig Show!

Susie's hair ribbon

Malcolm Carrick

Are you sitting comfortably? Then I'll begin.

One day Susie decided to put her new pink hair ribbon in her hair. She looked around her room, but she couldn't see it anywhere.

'Oh bother,' Susie said, 'I'm always losing things!'

So she looked under her bed. She didn't find her hair ribbon, but she found the lid of her jewel box.

'I've been looking for that,' said Susie, and she put the lid back on her jewel box.

Then she looked through all her drawers for her hair ribbon. She didn't find the pink ribbon,

36

but she did find five pence her aunt gave her last Christmas.

'I've been looking for that,' Susie said, and put it in her money box.

Then she looked under the carpet. She didn't find her hair ribbon, but she did find the key to her wind-up train.

'Oh, I've been looking for that,' she said as she put it with the train.

Next she turned out the wastepaper basket. Susie didn't find her hair ribbon, but she did find her doll's lost shoe.

'I've been looking for that,' she said, and put it on her doll's foot.

Susie thought her new pink hair ribbon might be in her school bag, so she turned that out. She didn't find the ribbon, but she did find the pencil sharpener she thought she had lost.

'I've been looking for that,' she said and went to put it in her school bag, but as it was there already, she went on searching for her hair ribbon.

'Perhaps it's in my doll's pram,' she thought, so she had a good rummage about in there. She didn't find the hair ribbon, but she did find the shiny medal her uncle had given her.

'I've been looking for that,' she said, and she put it in her doll's pram so that she would know where to find it again.

The last place she could think to look was in her toy box. She turned that out on the floor, but still she didn't find her hair ribbon. But she did find a frilly piece of lace that she'd been saving.

'I've been looking for that,' she said and put it in her sewing bag. Then she rushed downstairs.

'Mum,' she yelled, 'I've found the lid of my jewel box, and the key of my train, and five pence that Aunty gave me for Christmas, and my doll's shoe and my pencil sharpener, and Uncle's shiny medal, and my frilly piece of lace. But I still didn't find my new pink hair ribbon that I was looking for.'

'Well no wonder,' her Mum laughed. 'It's in your hair, Susie.'

Susie felt her hair, and there was the pink ribbon; it had been there all the time.

'I was looking for that,' she said.

Constantinople
or the elephant who
didn't like baths

Peter Ashley and Janey Gordon

Are you sitting comfortably? Then I'll begin.

Tom was playing in the living room, when an elephant's trunk came through the window.

'An elephant's trunk!' exclaimed Tom and, looking out of the window, he saw a small elephant.

'An elephant,' gasped Tom.

'What else do you expect to find at the end of a trunk?' said the elephant. 'My name is Constantinople.'

'I'm Tom,' said Tom. 'What are you doing here?'

'I've run away from the zoo, and you've got to hide me. My keeper will try to find me.'

Tom thought for a moment and then said, 'I've got some dressing-up clothes. Perhaps we could disguise you.'

Tom helped Constantinople in through the window.

'Shhhh, Constantinople, I don't want my

39

aunty to hear you,' said Tom. He was afraid that Aunty Alice, who was looking after him that day, might not be pleased by an elephant bouncing on to the sofa.

'Why have you run away?' Tom asked.

'I've got a new keeper and he makes me take a bath every day. I hate baths.'

'I know just how you feel,' agreed Tom.

Just then Constantinople saw his new keeper out in the street, coming towards the house.

'Quick,' he said, 'where's the disguise?'

'Here,' said Tom. 'Put on this bonnet and dress.'

Two minutes later the doorbell rang. Tom heard Aunty Alice open the door and a man's voice say, 'I saw my elephant coming this way. Do you mind if I look inside?'

Aunty Alice and the keeper came into the living room. Aunty Alice said to Tom, 'Have you seen an elephant?'

'I've been playing with my friend, Susan,' said Tom.

His 'friend Susan' was dressed in a big blue bonnet and a green dress with a gold belt.

'Bless my soul,' said the keeper. 'What big ears that girl's got.'

'It's very rude to make personal remarks,' said Aunty Alice, and they went out to look round the garden.

'Do you think he suspected?' said Constantinople as he took off the big blue bonnet.

'He might have,' said Tom. 'We'd better change your disguise. Put on Mummy's fur coat and stand on my skateboard.'

Two minutes later Tom heard Aunty Alice and the keeper come back into the house.

'Do you mind if I look in there again?' the keeper asked.

Aunty Alice and the keeper came into the living room. Aunty Alice said to Tom, 'Have you seen that elephant yet?'

'I've been playing with my toy dog, Woofa,' said Tom.

His 'toy dog Woofa' was brown and furry and was on wheels.

'Bless my soul,' said the keeper. 'What a long nose that dog's got.'

'They don't make toys like that any more,' said Aunty Alice, and they went out to look in the garage.

'Do you think he suspected?' said Constantinople as he took off Tom's mummy's fur coat.

'He might have,' said Tom. We'd better change your disguise. Put on this table cloth and kneel down.'

Two minutes later Tom heard Aunty Alice and the keeper come back into the house.

'Do you mind if I look in there one last time?'

the keeper asked.

Aunty Alice and the keeper came into the living room. Aunty Alice said to Tom, 'Any sign of that elephant yet?'

'I've been playing tea parties on my table,' said Tom.

His 'table' was a large lump with a red and white table-cloth on it, and a blue tea set all arranged for tea.

'Bless my soul,' said the keeper. 'What thick legs that table's got.'

'They don't make tables like that any more,' said Aunty Alice.

They were just going out to look in the kitchen when a big voice came from outside the window.

'Constantinople, Constantinople, where are you?'

When he heard this, Constantinople shouted, 'Mummy, Mummy,' and he rushed out from under the table-cloth, scattering the tea set all over the floor.

'I miss you, Mummy,' he cried as he bounced on the sofa, jumped out of the window and ran to his mummy, a large, grey elephant.

'Why did you run away?' his mummy said.

'I didn't want a bath every day,' said Constantinople.

Aunty Alice said, 'When Tom didn't like his baths, his mummy gave him some boats to play

42

with in the water.'

'What a good idea,' the keeper said.

So Constantinople borrowed some of Tom's boats to play with in his bath, and he became the cleanest elephant in the zoo!

Constantinople goes shopping

Peter Ashley and Janey Gordon

Are you sitting comfortably? Then I'll begin.

Tom had a special friend, Constantinople, who was a little elephant. One day Tom's Aunty Alice took Tom and Constantinople to do some shopping at the supermarket. On the supermarket door was a notice which said –

No Smoking
No Prams
No Dogs

'Upon my trunk,' Constantinople said. "No dogs.'

'That's all right,' said Tom. 'You're an elephant.'

44

Inside there were a lot of busy people carrying baskets or pushing their trolleys up and down the rows. Some mothers had their children in the trolleys.

'Can I have a ride?' Constantinople asked. And he climbed up on a trolley.

'You're too heavy,' said Tom. But it was too late.

CRRRRUNNNNCHHHHHHHH.

Constantinople squashed the trolley flat.

'Oh dear,' Aunty Alice sighed.

The supermarket manager, Mr Bargain-Price, came to see what the fuss was about.

'By Merthyr Tydfil!' he said. 'What a mess.'

'I'm sorry,' Constantinople said. 'I'll straighten it out.'

'And I'll help,' said Tom.

So they pulled and untwisted the wire trolley.

'I think I'll take a basket instead,' said Aunty Alice.

Tom asked Aunty Alice what was on her shopping list.

'The first thing,' she said, 'is a tin of baked beans.'

Constantinople looked along the shelf at all the different coloured tins.

'Here you are,' he said, going up to a tall stack of baked bean tins. He put out his trunk and, instead of taking a tin from the top, he took one from the bottom of the stack.

'Look out,' said Tom.

CRRRRRRAAAAASHHHHHH.

The whole lot came tumbling down and bounced all over the floor.

'Oh dear,' Aunty Alice sighed.

The supermarket manager, Mr Bargain-Price, came to see what the fuss was about.

'By Merthyr Tydfil and Abergavenny!' he said. 'What a mess.'

'I'm sorry,' Constantinople said. 'I'll pick them up.'

'And I'll help,' said Tom.

So they picked up all the tins and put them into a pile.

'I think I'll get spaghetti rings instead,' Aunty Alice said.

Tom asked Aunty Alice what was next on her shopping list.

'The second thing,' she said, 'is a packet of cornflakes.'

Constantinople looked along the shelf at all the different shaped packets.

'Here you are,' he said, picking up a packet. On the front of the packet it said 'Free Elephant'.

'Don't worry, elephant,' said Constantinople, 'I'll set you free. It's cruel to keep elephants in small boxes like that.'

RRRRRRRIPPPPPPPPPP.

He began to rip the box to pieces.

'It's only a tiny toy elephant that they give away free, for nothing,' said Tom.

The cornflakes were scattered about in the air like snow.

'Oh dear,' Aunty Alice sighed.

The supermarket manager, Mr Bargain-Price, came to see what the fuss was about.

'By Merthyr Tydfil, Abergavenny and Penrhyndeudraeth!' he said. 'What a mess.'

'I'm sorry,' Constantinople said. 'I'll clear it up.'

'And I'll help,' said Tom.

So they swept up all the cornflakes and bits of cardboard packet.

'I think I'll get porridge instead,' Aunty Alice said.

Tom asked Aunty Alice what was next on her shopping list.

'The third thing,' she said, 'is a box of soap powder.'

Constantinople looked along the shelf at all the different sized boxes.

'Here you are,' he said, picking up a very large box.

'That's much too big for me,' said Aunty Alice.

'It's just right for Constantinople,' Tom said. 'It's a jumbo pack!'

Just then, Mr Bargain-Price put on some

soothing music for his customers, to help them do their shopping.

'Upon my trunk,' yelled Constantinople, and leapt up into the air. 'Whenever I hear music I have to dance,' he said, grabbing Aunty Alice for a bossa nova.

Tom explained to the other customers that Constantinople's grandfather had been a circus elephant. That's why he was dancing.

'What a good idea,' they said. And soon all the other customers were doing the bossa nova too.

'Oh dear,' Aunty Alice panted.

The supermarket manager, Mr Bargain-Price, came to see what the fuss was about.

'By Merthyr Tydfil, Abergavenny, Penrhyn-deudraeth and Llanfairpwllgwyngyllgogerych-wyrndrobwllllantysiliogogogoch!!!' he said. 'This is too much.'

He went and turned the music off. Then he said to Aunty Alice, 'That elephant will have to go. At once. This instant. *Now*.'

Aunty Alice, Tom and Constantinople left.

They went home and they had tea. They were very hungry after all the dancing.

The next time Aunty Alice and Tom went to the supermarket, the notice on the door said –

No Smoking, No Prams, No Dogs, And Definitely *No Elephants*

Clever old foxy

Eugenie Summerfield

Are you sitting comfortably? Then I'll begin.

High up in the hills, quite hidden by the trees, lived an old foxy fox in his den. It was a lovely place to live. That old foxy fox could look down and see the stream where the ducks came to swim. He hardly ever came down to try and eat them! He would wink his eye and say,

'I bother nobody and nobody bothers me,
Because that's the way I like to be.'

Old Foxy was very happy with his way of life until one day along came a tickly, tetchy flea with his new little flea wife.

'Why my dear,' said Mr Flea to Mrs Flea, 'here's the very place for you and me to set up home and bring up a fine family.'

Together Mr Flea and Mrs Flea hopped up on old Foxy's back and settled down happily in the fox's warm golden fur.

At first old Foxy hardly noticed the fleas were there at all. He could still wink his eye and say,

'I bother nobody and nobody bothers me,
    Because that's the way I like to be.'

But after a while, there weren't just Mr Flea and Mrs Flea. There were hundreds of little fleas – all very naughty and very noisy. They hopped and they ran. From morning to night, they quarrelled and they fought. They played football and hide-and-seek. They held flea-circuses and flea-markets. They tickled and tormented that old Foxy from the top of his head to the tip of his tail.

Old Foxy tried to reason with them.

'Please go away,' he said. 'I bother nobody, so please don't bother me. That's the way I'd like to be.'

But those naughty fleas just laughed and said,

'Ha ha, hee hee! You won't get rid of us that easily!'

So old Foxy said to himself, 'I will have to think of some way of getting rid of these troublesome fleas.'

First he tried shaking himself very hard to make them all fall off, but they didn't. They all laughed and shouted,

'Ha ha, hee hee! You won't get rid of us so easily!'

Then he tried rolling in the sand to rub them out of his fur, but that didn't work either. Again they all laughed and shouted,

'Ha ha, hee hee! You won't get rid of us so easily!'

So old Foxy lay down among the long cool grasses. He stayed quite still until a bright idea came to him. Then he jumped up and ran around under the trees. In his mouth he gathered up all the soft green moss he could find.

The little fleas were much too busy being as naughty and as noisy as usual to notice what old Foxy was doing. Still carrying the soft green moss in his mouth, old Foxy went down through the trees until he came to the stream. The ducks swimming there were afraid old Foxy had come to eat them.

'Quack quack ducky dear, what shall we do?'

'Has old Foxy come to make a meal of me, or of you?'

But old Foxy didn't even look at the ducks. He turned his back upon them.

The ducks watched old Foxy walking backwards into the water carrying the moss in his mouth.

'Quack quack ducky dear, what is he up to?'

They decided it was safer for them not to stay. So the ducks flew away at once. Old Foxy waded deeper and deeper into the stream. The water nearly covered his back and all the naughty, noisy fleas on old Foxy's back shouted,

'Ha ha, hee hee! You won't get rid of us so easily!'

They hopped off old Foxy's back and up on to his nose.

But soon the water had reached old Foxy's nose. The fleas didn't like this one little bit. They ran round and round trying to keep out of the water. Until one of them saw the piece of moss in old Foxy's mouth.

'Look! If we all jump on to that soft green moss, we'll be as safe and snug as bugs in a rug. This old foxy fox can't get rid of us that easily!'

All together the fleas hopped on to the moss. Just as the very last one leapt off his nose, Old Foxy opened his mouth and let the moss, and all the fleas with it, float away down the stream.

He winked his eye and said,

'I bother nobody and nobody bothers me,
Because that's the way I like to be.'

Then he swam back to the water's edge. He climbed out and shook himself dry. Old Foxy went back to his den among the hills where he danced and sang all by himself in the sunlight.

The dog who had
no name
Leila Berg

Are you sitting comfortably? Then I'll begin.

Once upon a time there was a dog.

He was a very jolly dog, a yellow dog, and his nose was black. He had two white paws and two brown paws. But he had no name at all. One day this little yellow dog said to himself, 'Everybody has a name but me. I shall go off and find a name.' So off he went. Patter, patter, patter, patter on his neat little feet.

He pattered down the street, and he passed some men mending the road. 'Hello, little yellow dog,' shouted the road men. 'Where are you off to, in such a hurry?'

'I'm off to find my name,' said the little yellow dog.

'Stop a minute,' cried the road men. 'Is Pat your name?'

'No, Pat isn't my name,' said the little yellow dog. And on he went. Patter, patter, patter, patter on his neat little feet.

He pattered down the street, till he passed a lady buying bread. 'Hello little yellow dog,' said the lady. 'Where are you running so far away?'

'I'm off to find my name,' said the little yellow dog.

'Wait a bit,' cried the lady. 'Is Bess your name?'

'Oh no, Bess isn't my name,' said the little yellow dog. And on he went. Patter, patter, patter, patter on his neat little feet.

On he pattered till he came to a window-cleaner, carrying a ladder. 'Hello, little yellow dog,' cried the window-cleaner. 'Where are you off to, this fine day?'

'I'm off to find my name,' said the little yellow dog.

'Don't go so fast,' said the window-cleaner. 'Is Gyp your name?'

'No, Gyp isn't my name,' said the little yellow dog. And on he went. Patter, patter, patter, patter on his neat little feet.

On he pattered till he came to a postman carrying letters. 'Hello little yellow dog,' said the postman. 'Where are you going, at such a rate?'

'I'm going to find my name,' said the little yellow dog.

'Is Rough your name?' asked the postman.

'No, Rough isn't my name,' said the little yellow dog. And on he went. Patter, patter, patter, patter on his neat little feet. On he pattered till he was tired out. Then he sat down on the pavement at the side of the road, and he stuck out his tongue.

And he huffed, and he huffed, and he huffed.

'Oh!' he said – 'OH-oh-oh. I'll – never – never – never – never – find – my – name. Oh-oh-oh.'

Just then two little children came along. A boy and a girl. 'Hello, little yellow dog,' said the boy and girl. 'You look quite tired out. Whatever have you been doing?'

'Huff, huff, huff,' said the little yellow dog, 'I've been looking for my name – huff – but I haven't found it yet – huff – and I'm very tired – huff, huff, huff.'

'Wait a minute,' said the children. 'Don't go away. Is Trix your name? Is it Trix?'

The little dog thought for a moment. First he put his head on one side and thought that way. Then he put his head on the other side, and thought that way. Then he stood up and wagged his tail. Then he turned round quickly three times and barked, yap, yap.

'Yes,' he said. 'It *is*. Trix *is* my name. Yap, yap!'

'Hooray,' shouted the children. 'Then you can come with us. Come on, Trix.'

And off they ran, shouting and singing and barking. The little girl, the little boy and the little yellow dog.

Fingy and the garden

Diana Webb

Are you sitting comfortably? Then I'll begin.

Susie's favourite toy was a little woolly man who fitted neatly on her finger. His name was Fingy and he had yellow hair and a blue and red striped suit.

One afternoon Susie went for a walk in the country with Fingy in her pocket. She skipped along behind Mummy and Daddy as they rambled through a wood, down a hill with cottages on either side and into a leafy lane. When they turned the corner at the end of the lane they began to walk beside a long high wall built of red brick.

'What's on the other side of that wall, Daddy?' asked Susie.

'Someone's garden and house I expect,' said Daddy.

'It must be a very big garden. Does the Queen live there?' asked Susie.

'I don't think so,' said Daddy.

'If you lifted me up on your shoulder,' said Susie, 'I think I would be able to see into the garden.'

'Oh no,' said Daddy firmly. 'I can't do that. That would be nosey.'

Susie was very disappointed. Mummy and Daddy walked a little further and sat down for a rest on the grass by the side of the road while Susie dawdled along looking up at the wall.

Suddenly she saw a very long twig lying on the ground and she had a wonderful idea. She took Fingy out of her pocket and said, 'Fingy, I'm going to put you on the end of this twig and then I'm going to stand on tiptoe and hold the twig as high above my head as I can, so you will be able to see over the wall and tell me what is on the other side.'

'I don't want to be nosey,' said Fingy uncertainly.

'It's all right,' said Susie. 'That little bird sitting on the wall can see into the garden, but he isn't being nosey is he?'

'Isn't he?' said Fingy.

'No of course not,' said Susie. 'Come on Fingy.'

She fitted him on to the end of the twig and held it up in the air. Then she stood on tiptoe and stretched as high as she could.

'Can you see over the wall, Fingy?' she asked breathlessly.

'Just about,' said Fingy.

'What can you see?' asked Susie, feeling very excited.

'I can see a man mowing the lawn with a shiny silver lawnmower,' said Fingy.

'And what else?' gasped Susie.

'I can see a big tree with beautiful red flowers shaped like bells. There are four people sitting under the tree in wicker chairs, eating enormous gigantic strawberries.'

'Who are they?' cried Susie. 'Tell me who they are.'

'There is a pirate. He is feeding his parrot with one of the strawberries. Next to him there is a clown. He is sticking one of the strawberries on the end of his nose. And next to him there is a wizard. He is waving his hands over one of the strawberries. I think he is trying to change it into something.'

'Is there anyone else?' squeaked Susie.

'There is a lady, she is eating her strawberries sensibly,' said Fingy.

'Who is the lady? Is it the Queen?' Susie was so excited that she jumped up and down. 'Is it the Queen, Fingy? Is it the Queen?'

Before Fingy could answer, Susie jumped up and down so much that she tossed poor Fingy right off the top of the twig, over the wall and into the garden.

She stared for a long time at the bare end of the twig where Fingy had been sitting. Then she started to cry. She cried and she cried until suddenly she saw something shoot up above the top of the wall. When she rubbed her tears away she saw that somebody on the other side of the wall had lifted a twig high in the air, and Fingy was perched on top of it. Susie quickly picked up her own twig, raised it up to the wall and carefully hoisted Fingy off the end of the other person's twig. Soon she was clutching Fingy tightly in her hand again.

She stared at the wall and opened her mouth to say to the person on the other side, 'Are you the Queen?' but she was too shy, so she just whispered, 'Thank you very much,' and ran to find her Mummy and Daddy.

When she stopped running she said to Fingy, 'Was it the Queen in that garden?' Fingy moved his head, but Susie wasn't quite sure whether he meant 'Yes' or 'No'.

Fingy and the magic stone

Diana Webb

Are you sitting comfortably? Then I'll begin.

One afternoon when the sun was shining, Susie went to some woods for a picnic. In the woods there was a stone that was as big as a car. It was covered in moss and it looked like a huge grey and green frog.

'Do you think that's a magic stone?' Susie asked her Daddy.

'I don't know,' said Daddy, 'I suppose it might be.'

'But do you think it is?' said Susie.

'I really don't know,' said Daddy.

Susie walked up to the stone. She walked

round it but she was careful not to touch it. Then she hid behind the stone and took Fingy out of her pocket.

'If you touch that stone you're silly,' she told him.

'Why?' said Fingy.

'Because it's a magic stone,' said Susie.

'I don't mind touching it,' said Fingy.

'But it might put a spell on you,' said Susie.

'It might put a *good* spell on me,' said Fingy.

Susie looked at the stone and she looked at Fingy. 'Are you sure you don't mind touching it?' she said.

'I don't mind at all,' said Fingy.

Susie started to pull Fingy off her finger, but she didn't pull him right off. She pulled him until only his feet were touching the end of her finger. Then she reached out slowly, and very quickly she touched the stone with the top of Fingy's head. For a moment she was frightened that he might disappear, but he just smiled back at Susie.

'It didn't hurt,' said Fingy. 'I feel all special and magic now.'

Susie ran to her Daddy.

'Fingy touched the magic stone,' she shouted.

'Did he really?' said Daddy.

'Yes he did,' said Susie, 'so do you think he's lucky now?'

'I have no idea,' said Daddy.

'How can I find out?' asked Susie.

'I don't know,' said Daddy.

Susie stared at Fingy and Fingy stared at Susie and they both thought very hard.

'Point me straight ahead of you,' said Fingy, 'and I'll lead you to some treasure.'

So Susie pointed Fingy in front of her and they went for a walk among the trees. They walked round and round in circles.

'Why are we walking round and round in circles?' said Susie.

'We're looking for treasure,' said Fingy.

'I don't think that stone made you lucky at all,' said Susie. 'I don't think that you're going to find anything.'

'Yes I am,' said Fingy. 'You must shut your eyes now, and turn round three times with your arms stretched out, and when you stop you must look where I'm pointing and walk three steps in that direction.'

Susie did as she was told, but she couldn't see any treasure when she stopped.

'Now you must do it again,' said Fingy.

So Susie did it again, but she still couldn't see any treasure.

'*And* you must do it again,' said Fingy.

So Susie did it once more.

'I'm pointing straight to the treasure now,' said Fingy, 'but you might have to walk a long way to find it.'

Susie sighed. Very slowly she followed Fingy in a straight line. She had to walk slowly because she was staring at the ground.

'What are you doing?' said Daddy.

'Ssh,' said Susie. 'I'm looking for treasure.' She bent nearer and nearer to the ground until she was pushing Fingy along on the path. The top of his head became rather dirty.

'Look,' said Fingy suddenly. 'I've found it.'

There on the ground in front of him was a shiny silver fifty-pence piece.

Susie was very excited. She gazed at the fifty-pence piece. Then she picked it up.

'The stone did make you lucky Fingy,' she said. 'It must have been magic.'

'Fingys are *always* lucky,' said Fingy.

A hat for Bethan

Gill Davies

Are you sitting comfortably? Then I'll begin.

Bethan wanted a hat. She watched the postman with his smart, peaked cap as he pushed letters through the letter-boxes all along the road.

'Can I have a hat, please?' she said.

Mummy was washing up. She popped a plastic cup upside down on Bethan's head.

'There,' she said, 'a hat!'

But Bethan knew that wouldn't do. So she shook her head – and the plastic cup fell, clatter bang, on to the kitchen floor.

'I would like a hat,' said Bethan, as they sat on the bus, going to visit Gran. The bus driver had a lovely blue squashy hat with a red edge – and a money bag, too. Mummy smiled. She tied her scarf round Bethan's head.

'There,' she said, 'a hat!'

But the knot hurt Bethan's neck and she knew that wouldn't do.

'Please give me a hat,' said Bethan, as they sat

drinking tea at Gran's. Grandpa folded his newspaper into a triangle and popped it on Bethan's head.

'There,' he said, 'a hat!'

But when Bethan stood up the hat slipped right down over her nose and she trod on the cat. That wouldn't do, either.

'Please can I try on your hat?' Bethan asked a policeman in town, but the policeman said sadly he wasn't allowed to take it off, that it was far too heavy anyway, and that it made even his strong head ache by the end of the day.

'Please can I try on your hat?' Bethan asked the chef in the café.

'It's far too full of flour,' he wheezed. He shook his head, and great clouds of white dust flew into the air and made Bethan sneeze.

'Please can I try on your hat?' Bethan asked the fireman.

'Oh no, my lovely,' said the fireman, 'I keep my sandwiches inside it!' And he raised his helmet to show Bethan his lunch.

'I want a hat,' said Bethan.

'I know,' said Mummy.

'Say "please",' said Daddy.

'Please,' said Bethan.

'Well, here you are then!' said Mummy.

And there, in Mummy's hand, was a beautiful blue and red striped hat, with a white fluffy pom-

pom on the top. At last! A hat for Bethan.

'I've got a hat,' said Bethan.

'I've got a hat,' said Bethan, to everyone she saw.

'I know,' said the postman.

'I know,' said the bus conductor.

'I know,' said Gran, and Grandpa, and the policeman, and the chef, and the fireman, 'I know, and a fine hat it is too, Bethan. Aren't you lucky?'

'Fraidy mouse

Anne Wellington

Are you sitting comfortably? Then I'll begin.

Once upon a time there were three grey mice. And they lived in a corner of a barn.

Two of the mice weren't afraid of anything, except the brown tabby cat who lived in the farmhouse. Two of the mice said, 'Hi! Look at us. We're tricky and we're quicky and we're fighty and we're bitey. We're not afraid of anything, except the tabby cat.'

But the third little mouse said, 'Don't look at me. I'm quivery and quaky and shivery and shaky. I'm afraid of everything. I'm a 'Fraidy Mouse.'

'Fraidy Mouse's brothers said, 'Don't be

ridiculous. There's nothing to be frightened of, except the tabby cat.'

'Fraidy Mouse shivered, 'I've never seen a tabby cat. Does Tabby Cat stamp with his feet? Does he growl?'

'Fraidy Mouse's brothers said, 'Don't be absurd. Tabby Cat sits by the door of the barn.

> He sits on the ground,
> He's big and he's round.
> He doesn't move a muscle
> Till he hears a little rustle.
> Then he'll jump. Thump!
> And he'll eat you till you're dead.'

Then 'Fraidy Mouse's brothers said, 'But Tabby Cat's indoors now. So off we go together to be bold, brave mice.'

'Fraidy Mouse was left alone, sitting in the barn. In case he should see something fearsome and frightening, he closed his eyes tightly and fell fast asleep.

While 'Fraidy Mouse was sleeping, the farmer passed the barn. He was carrying a sack full of big brown potatoes. One of the potatoes fell out and rolled about. It rolled to the door of the barn. And there it stayed.

'Fraidy Mouse woke up. He saw that big potato! 'Mercy me! It's Tabby Cat, sitting by the door!

He's sitting on the ground,
And he's big and he's round.
He won't move a muscle
Till he hears a little rustle.
Then he'll jump. Thump!
And he'll eat me till I'm dead.'

'Fraidy Mouse kept so still that all his bones were aching. Then his brothers came back, and they said, 'Hi, 'Fraidy Mouse!'

'Fraidy Mouse whispered, 'Hush! Oh hush! Don't you see the tabby cat sitting by the door?'

'Fraidy Mouse's brothers said, 'Don't be idiotic. That's not a tabby cat. That's a big potato.' And they laughed. 'Fraidy Mouse's brothers rolled around laughing, until they were exhausted and had to go to sleep.

But poor little 'Fraidy Mouse cried himself to sleep.

While the mice were sleeping, the farmer passed the barn. He picked the potato up and carried it away. 'Fraidy Mouse twitched in his sleep – dreaming. He dreamed he was a tricky, quicky little mouse.

As the sun went down, the big brown tabby cat came padding to the barn. And he sat by the door. 'Fraidy Mouse twitched in his sleep again – dreaming. He dreamed he was a fighty, bitey little mouse.

After a while, the mice woke up. The first thing

they saw in the twilight was the cat, a big round brown thing sitting by the door. 'Fraidy Mouse's brothers hid away in holes. They stared out with frightened eyes, too terrified to speak.

'Fraidy Mouse thought they were teasing him again, pretending to be frightened of a big brown potato. He wouldn't get caught like *that* again!

He called out, 'Hi there! You silly old potato!' The tabby cat was so surprised he didn't move a muscle. 'Fraidy Mouse called again, 'I'm only small and 'Fraidy. But I'm not afraid of *you*, you silly old potato. And neither are my tricky, quicky, fighty, bitey brothers.'

Tabby Cat said to himself, 'What a mouse! If that's a little 'Fraidy Mouse, the smallest, most afraid mouse, his brothers must be terrible. I shan't come here again'.

Then Tabby Cat stalked away, pretending not to hurry. And 'Fraidy Mouse said, 'Funny! That potato's got a tail!'

'Fraidy Mouse's tricky, quicky, fighty, bitey brothers came creeping from their holes, and they said, 'Oh 'Fraidy Mouse! How brave you were to talk to the tabby cat like that!'

'Fraidy Mouse thought, 'Tabby Cat! That wasn't a potato. I was talking to a real live tabby cat. Oh my!'

Then his legs gave way, and he fell on his back. And his brothers said, 'He's resting. It's tiring being so brave!'

The ballad of Bad Belinda

Moira Miller

Are you sitting comfortably? Then I'll begin.

I'll tell you a story, I promise it's true,
Of a Horrible Child – it couldn't be you!
Her name was Belinda Samantha de Vere,
And her Terrible Tale is quite shocking to hear.

Now Belinda was known the length of the street
As the sort of child you would *hate* to meet,
And mothers would say as they saw her pass by,
'There's Dreadful Belinda! I simply must fly
To take in the cat, or she'll start having fits.
Belinda has frightened her out of her wits!'
For that Terrible Child was a *most awful tease,*
And actually thought it 'a jolly good wheeze'
To tie an old tin to the long furry tail
Of a cat who lay sleeping on top of the wall.
She would then yell 'Ya-Boo!' at the top of her
  voice,
And up leapt the cat – what a horrible noise!

Clanking and banging and yowling and screaming.
She thought it was funny, and found it quite
  pleasing
That people were so upset by her teasing.
She pestered the Baby, asleep in his pram;
Stuffed a hairbrush in bed with her Big Brother
  Sam,
Who woke with a start and jumped out with a
  yell,
'There's a hedgehog in bed! I know I can tell.
I felt all its bristles. I'm sure that it wiggled!'
Dreadful Belinda just giggled and giggled.

Her mother would scold and her father would
  shout,
But that Horrible Child was never put out.
She went on and on being Dreadfully Naughty,
Until the arrival of – Great Aunt Dotty.

This lady arrived on the doorstep one day,
And announced to the Family, 'I'm coming to
  stay.
The doctor has told me to have a good rest,
And a peaceful holiday here would be best.'
Now Belinda's Mum didn't have a Great Aunt,
And her Father, when questioned, admitted, 'I
  can't
Recall any mention of such a relation.
However she's here, and her bag's at the station.'

So they sent for her luggage and round came a
    porter,
A stout chap with whiskers, who said, 'I ain't
    never
Seen a lady wiv so much stuff!
There's 'at boxes, suit-cases, trunks and a muff
Of 'orrible fur – striped black, white and tan.'
'That's my cat,' said Aunt Dotty, 'you Foolish
    Young Man!'
'A cat!' thought Belinda: that Terrible Infant
Was planning all sorts of tricks in an instant.
She smiled at the cat with a horrible leer,
But the animal simply replied with a sneer.
He stretched and yawned a most elegant yawn,
And curled up to sleep on the front garden lawn.

Aunt Dotty by now was enjoying a cuppa
And ordering sardines on toast for her supper.
It was whilst she was nibbling at this tasty snack
That Belinda crept up to the room at the back,
The second-best bedroom – reserved for a guest.
(Belinda's Mother and Dad had the best!)
Here were Aunt Dotty's bags, all neatly stacked,
None of them being, as yet, unpacked.
Belinda – Bad Child – can you guess what she
    did?
Saw that hat-box on top, so she lifted the lid,
Intending, I'm sure there's no doubt of that,
To hide her pet mouse in Aunt Dotty's best hat.

But she dropped the lid with a terrible shout
As a huge hairy Jack-In-The-Box shot out!
Mother and Dad heard the rumpus of course,
And rushed up the stairs to discover the source.
Aunt Dotty just smiled and hitched up her cloak,
And muttered, 'What? Can't the child take a
  joke?'

Next morning at breakfast Belinda sat down
To a large boiled egg, a most beautiful brown.
Freckled and speckled, it looked really good.
A tasty boiled egg was her favourite food.
She picked up her spoon and tapped on the shell –
It was empty inside! Aunt Dotty said, 'Well!
Now there's a surprise you didn't foresee.
Just one of my little jokes. Now have some tea.'
But the cup that she handed that Terrible Child
Was salted, not sugared, and oh how she wailed!
Her Big Brother Sam, getting on with his meal,
Said, 'Serves you quite right. Now you know how
  we feel
When we have to put up with the tricks that *you*
  play.'
At this Our Belinda had nothing to say.

She stamped out to the shed feeling wickedly
  Naughty,
To plan her revenge on Great Aunt Dotty.
She was sitting there thinking some Terrible
  Thinks

When a dirty great spider came down through
  the chinks
In the roof of that rickety old garden shed.
It landed – precisely – on top of her head.
Belinda sat, terrified, fixed to her stool,
Till she noticed a label that read APRIL FOOL!
There was also another with MADE IN HONG
  KONG.
That spider was plastic! Could he belong
To Aunt Dotty's collection of Horrible Tricks?
'You bet,' groaned Belinda, and wondered,
  'What next?'

The week dragged on getting worse and worse.
Great Aunt Dot was a Terrible Curse.
Belinda discovered her shoes full of jam,
And a wheel unscrewed from the Baby's pram
When Belinda was taking him out for his walk.
She'd to carry him home, which wasn't a joke!
The Baby, you see, didn't like being carried,
And wanted to crawl, so he struggled and
  worried
And pulled at her pigtails till, all in a muddle,
Belinda and Baby both fell in a puddle.
They struggled back home, very tired and dirty,
And Belinda's Mum was really quite shirty.

At last, at the end of this Terrible Week,
Belinda was feeling thoroughly sick.
'If only she'd *go*,' wailed the Poor Child in pain,

'I'd never tease anyone EVER AGAIN!'
(Aunt Dotty had planted a drawing-pin
On the seat of her chair before she came in.)
'Did I hear aright?' said Great Aunt Dot.
'You'll never tease anyone – even the cat?'
'Oh Truly, Aunt Dot!' sobbed Belinda, and so
Aunt Dot went upstairs and got ready to go.

'But always remember,' she said as she packed,
'Any more nonsense and – *I'll be right back*!'

The giant brothers
and the army

Val Annan

Are you sitting comfortably? Then I'll begin.

Giant Huster and Giant Bluster were twin brothers who were very wicked – they were always up to naughty tricks. One day, when they had been very, very bad, they were caught by the scruff of their necks and thrown out of Giantland!

'Be off with you, you terrible twins – and don't bother to come back until you are nice giants!' the other giants said.

'Bah!' yelled Huster and Bluster angrily, as they stamped away.

At first, the twin giants had a wonderful time – tearing up trees, blocking up streams and rivers and causing no end of wicked damage everywhere they went. Then, one day at around four o'clock when all good giants were at home having their tea, Huster and Bluster stood on top of a cold mountain. Far below them, they saw a little town where little people were hurrying this way and that.

Huster yelled at them, 'Hey! You down there . . . . Look at us! We are Giants Huster and Bluster!'

'And we want out tea!' said Bluster. 'Send it up to us or it will be the worse for you! We want two hundred boiled eggs, four hundred slices of buttered toast and ninety-three buckets of tea!'

The people in the little town quickly gathered around their Lord Mayor.

'What can we do?' they wailed. 'Our town isn't big enough to have such giant visitors – they will eat us out of house and home.'

The Lord Mayor looked thoughtful. 'We must give them their tea, or they might eat us! Perhaps they'll go away if we give them what they want!'

So, Huster and Bluster sat on top of the mountain and they had two hundred boiled eggs, four hundred slices of buttered toast and ninety-three buckets of tea.

'Hmm . . . that's better,' said Huster smacking his lips and rubbing his tummy.

'But we'll want the same again for breakfast

tomorrow – and a roast turkey lunch!' said Bluster.

'I'm afraid that isn't possible,' replied the little Mayor. 'Our food is needed for our um . . . Army!'

'Army!' roared Huster. 'I see no soldiers!'

'No, I see no soldiers and that means there is no Army!' said Bluster.

'Our soldiers are away at the moment – giant hunting – but they'll be back tomorrow – so you'd better be off while you can,' said the little Mayor.

'Bah!' said Huster.

'Bah!' said Bluster. 'We don't believe you. We shall wait to see this army of yours. But now, we'll have a good night's sleep in this big cave on your mountain. Be off with you! Army indeed!'

So the little people went back to the town and looked sadly at the Mayor.

'Where can we get an Army from at such short notice?' they wailed.

The Lord Mayor sighed, and looked up at the wintry sky. A big white snowflake drifted down and touched him lightly on the nose.

'Why! It's snowing!' he laughed. 'Quickly, everyone get out your shovels and spades – we must all make ten snowmen!'

And the little people worked all through the night – building snowmen!

Then they got out their pots of paint and they painted uniforms on the snowmen! The people gave them sticks and broom handles for guns.

Next morning when Huster and Bluster woke up they could hardly believe their eyes. All over the town and at the foot of the mountain were soldiers in red and white uniforms! They were all holding guns and did not look at all friendly.

Of course the twin giants didn't realize the soldiers were only made of snow.

'The Army is here!' gasped Huster. 'There are hundreds and hundreds of soldiers down there!'

Very frightened, Bluster said, 'I'm going back to Giantland this minute!'

'So am I!' said Huster.

And the giants twins ran all the way home.

They banged hard on the gates to Giantland, squealing, 'Please let us in – the Army is after us . . . please let us in!'

'Only if you promise to be good giants from now on,' said a booming voice from behind the gate.

'We promise! We promise!' squealed Huster and Bluster.

And they were good from that day on!

Young hedgehog helps rabbit

Vera Rushbrooke

Are you sitting comfortably? Then I'll begin.

Young Hedgehog and Rabbit were sitting by the hedge in the freshness of the early morning. Drops of dew were sparkling in the cobwebs stretched along the hedge, the birds were singing and everything was lovely.

Rabbit was saying, 'I feel so tired today! I don't know why. I don't work hard like Mole, digging out all those tunnels of his. And I don't run for miles like Red Fox when the dogs are after him. I don't even trot round the field like you do.'

'In fact,' chuckled Young Hedgehog, 'you're a lazy sort of fellow! Still, it's nice lazing about sometimes and listening to the bees humming, and smelling the honeysuckle in the hedge and the meadowsweet in the ditch, and just looking at things. Perhaps you feel tired because it's that sort of a morning, or maybe you didn't sleep well.'

'The trouble is,' said Rabbit, 'I heard there are

some nice juicy dandelions at the end of the next field, and I did fancy some. There aren't any around here. But I'm just too tired to go all that way.'

'You know,' said Young Hedgehog, 'once I felt like going for a trot to the wood, but it's rather a long way and I was tired, so I closed my eyes and *imagined* I went to the wood.

I kept talking to myself like this – Now I'm trotting over the daisy field till I come to the gate. Now I'm squeezing through the hedge where Mother Blackbird has her nest – and so on, till I *imagined* I'd got to the wood. It seemed so *real*, and all the time there I was sitting by the hedge with my eyes closed! Why don't you try it?'

'You really felt you'd been there?' asked Rabbit, 'just by closing your eyes and *thinking* it?'

'Yes,' said Young Hedgehog. 'You try it. Go on, sit down and close your eyes.'

'All right,' said Rabbit, and he sat down and closed his eyes.

'Now,' said Young Hedgehog, 'you want to go to the end of the next field, that's right?'

'Yes,' said Rabbit.

'Right,' said Young Hedgehog. 'Now, you know the way, so off we go, hoppity hop, over the daisy field.'

'Over the daisy field,' said Rabbit, with his eyes shut tight.

'And now,' Young Hedgehog said, 'you've got to the hedge. Can you squeeze through into the next field?'

'Yes,' said Rabbit, screwing up his nose as though he was trying hard.

'Are you through?' asked Young Hedgehog.

'Yes,' said Rabbit.

'Bit of a tough job, that, wasn't it?' Young Hedgehog said. 'Never mind, you're through now and in the next field. It's going to be difficult because the farmer's tractor has been over it, but off we go, hoppity hop!'

'Hoppity hop,' said Rabbit, his eyes tightly shut and not moving an inch.

'How rough the soil is now the tractor has turned it over,' said Young Hedgehog. 'Would you rather go round by the hedge?'

'It would be easier,' said Rabbit.

'Right!' said Young Hedgehog. 'Off we go.'

'Off we go!' Rabbit said, screwing up his eyes and imagining.

'Nearly there now,' said Young Hedgehog, 'mind you don't fall over the branches the wind has blown from the sycamore tree.'

'Right!' said Rabbit.

'Here we are,' said Young Hedgehog, 'at the end of the next field, where you wanted to go.'

'Can I open my eyes now?' asked Rabbit.

'No!' cried Young Hedgehog. 'You've got to go

back home. Come on, round by the hedge again. Mind the branches! Big ones, aren't they?'

'Yes,' Rabbit said, still with his eyes closed tight.

'Now, squeeze back through the hedge into the daisy field again,' said Young Hedgehog. 'Are you through?'

'Yes,' said Rabbit.

'Good!' Young Hedgehog said. 'Now over the daisy field and back home.'

'Can I open my eyes now?' asked Rabbit.

'Oh yes,' said Young Hedgehog.

Rabbit opened his eyes and blinked in the light.

'That was easy, wasn't it?' chuckled Young Hedgehog.

'Yes,' laughed Rabbit. 'All that way, and I didn't move an inch!' But suddenly he stopped laughing and began to look angry.

'What's the matter?' asked Young Hedgehog.

'What's the matter?' stormed Rabbit. 'I'll tell you what's the matter! We forgot the dandelions! That's all I wanted to go for!' And Rabbit hopped off to look for something to eat, muttering to himself, 'That Young Hedgehog and his stupid ideas!'

While Young Hedgehog just chuckled and said, 'I only tried to help!'

Teddy bear gets too fat
for his jacket

Margaret Gore

Are you sitting comfortably? Then I'll begin.

One morning when Teddy Bear was doing up his dark blue jacket with the three brass buttons, one of the buttons popped off and fell on the floor. It was the middle button.

'Oh dear,' said Teddy Bear in his deep, growly voice. 'I must be getting fat.'

He looked at himself in the mirror.

'Either I have got fat or the jacket has shrunk. Perhaps it shrank when I got caught in all that rain the other day.' Then Teddy Bear remembered he had been wearing his green pullover that day. So it wasn't that.

'There is no doubt about it,' said Teddy Bear. 'I have got too fat, and I shall have to do some exercises.'

But by the time Teddy Bear had done arms stretch three times, and knees bend twice, he was quite out of breath. 'Oh dear,' he growled. '*That* won't do. I shall have to think of something else. Perhaps my friend Badger, who lives on the common, can help me.'

So down to the common went Teddy Bear – left, right, left, right, left, right. He found Badger busily digging in the earth.

'Please, Badger, can you help me?' asked Teddy Bear. 'I have got too fat and I can't do up my jacket.'

'You should try digging holes as I do, Teddy Bear,' said Badger, and went on with his digging.

So Teddy Bear took off his jacket with the two buttons on instead of three, and began digging. He was tired out after digging up only about one pailful of earth.

'Oh dear,' growled Teddy Bear. '*That* won't do. I don't think bears are meant to dig holes. I'll have to think of something else. Perhaps my friend Brown Dog, who lives at the crossroads, can help me.'

So off went Teddy Bear again, left, right, left, right, till he came to the crossroads. Brown Dog lived in the house on the corner, and there he was, running about in his big garden.

'Please can you help me, Brown Dog?' asked
Teddy Bear. 'I have got too fat and I can't do up
my jacket.'

'You should do as I do, Teddy Bear,' replied
Brown Dog. 'I am always running about – I
hardly ever stop, except when I go to bed.'

So Teddy Bear ran all the way home without
stopping once for a rest, but when he arrived he
was so breathless he had to sit down in his
armchair and have a few spoonfuls from a tin of
sweet milk to make him feel better.

'Oh dear,' growled Teddy Bear. '*That* won't do.
I don't think bears are meant to keep on running
all the time without stopping. I'll have to think of
something else. Perhaps my friend Tabcat will be
able to help me.'

Down the road he went again, left, right, left,
right, till he came to Tabcat's house. He saw
Tabcat sitting on top of the high wall that went
round his garden.

'Can you help me, Tabcat?' asked Teddy Bear.
'I have got too fat and I can't do up my jacket.'

'You should try jumping, Teddy Bear,' replied
Tabcat, looking down at him with his green eyes.
'I am always jumping up on to this wall.'

'Jumping?' said Teddy Bear, doubtfully.

Tabcat looked at Teddy Bear's fat little figure
standing there, and he said kindly, 'Perhaps you

should start jumping on to *little* walls first, Teddy Bear. Come with me – I'll show you where there's one.'

Tabcat jumped gracefully down from the high wall and led Teddy Bear into the rose-garden.

'There you are, Teddy Bear, there's a nice *low* wall,' said Tabcat. 'Now if you'll excuse me, it's time for my lunch.'

It may have been a low wall to Tabcat, but to Teddy Bear it looked quite high. However, he went back a few steps, then took a flying leap at the wall. Unfortunately he didn't jump quite high enough, and he landed on the ground with a hard thud.

'Ooooo! Oh dear,' growled Teddy Bear. 'I *certainly* don't think bears were meant to go jumping up on to walls – even if they are only low ones.'

He walked sadly back home, feeling rather stiff and sore. On the way he came to Mrs Duck's shop. Once a week he always bought a large jar of honey at Mrs Duck's shop, and today was the day for it.

'It's no use,' he said to himself. 'The only way I shall stop being fat is to give up eating sweet things. I must go in and tell Mrs Duck that I shall not be needing any more jars of honey. Oh dear!'

He gave a big sigh, for if there was one thing Teddy Bear did love it was honey. But he bravely pushed open the shop door and went in.

'My goodness, Teddy Bear, you do look tired,' exclaimed Mrs Duck, and she made him sit down on a chair.

'I do feel rather weak, Mrs Duck,' replied Teddy Bear, and he cast a longing glance at a jar of honey on the shelf.

'Poor Teddy Bear, you probably need something to eat. I'll give you a big cup of cocoa and a chocolate biscuit. Then you'll feel better.'

Teddy Bear held up a weak paw.

'No, no thank you, Mrs Duck, I won't have anything,' he said. 'Not *anything*.'

Mrs Duck stared at Teddy Bear in astonishment.

'You must be ill, Teddy Bear,' she said. 'Perhaps I should call the doctor?'

Then Teddy Bear told her all his troubles, and showed her his jacket. 'The middle button came right off this morning,' he said, 'because I am getting too fat.'

'Nonsense, Teddy Bear,' laughed Mrs Duck. 'It only means you are growing up into a fine big bear – and who ever heard of a *thin* bear?

'Now you just stay there, and while you're drinking that cup of cocoa and eating that chocolate biscuit I shall sew your buttons on in a different place. Then you will be able to do up your jacket quite easily, I'm sure. I hope you haven't lost that middle button, Teddy Bear?'

'Oh no, Mrs Duck,' replied Teddy Bear. 'Here it is in my pocket.'

Mrs Duck sewed the buttons on one inch nearer to the edge.

'Now, Teddy Bear,' she said. 'Come and try your jacket on.'

It fitted perfectly.

'Oh, thank you, Mrs Duck,' cried Teddy Bear. 'Now I must go home – and I'll take a jar of honey with me – a large jar.'

When Teddy Bear arrived home he put the jar of honey on the table and took out a big spoon.

Then he gave a deep, growly laugh.

'Who ever heard of a *thin* bear?' he said.

Alison's new baby

Shelley R. Lee

Are you sitting comfortably? Then I'll begin.

One day Alison came downstairs to see what Mummy was doing. She wasn't in the kitchen. She wasn't in the dining room. She wasn't outside hanging out the washing. Then Alison found her. She was in the garage, with a bowl of water and a cloth, washing Alison's old pram, the one with the big wheels.

'What are you doing, Mummy?' asked Alison.

'I'm washing your old pram,' said Mummy.

'Yes,' said Alison. 'But *why* are you washing my old pram? I'm much too big to ride in it now.'

'Well,' said Mummy, 'I thought maybe we would have a new baby to put in it soon.'

So Alison helped to wash the pram, and Mummy said, 'When the new baby comes, you will be my big girl, and help to push the pram.'

Now the next day Alison came downstairs to see what Mummy was doing. She wasn't in the kitchen. She wasn't in the dining room. She wasn't outside hanging out the washing. Then Alison found her. She was in the smallest bedroom, with a bowl of water and a cloth, wiping down Alison's old baby bath.

'What are you doing, Mummy?' asked Alison.

'I'm wiping down your old baby bath,' said Mummy.

'Yes,' said Alison. 'But *why* are you wiping down my old baby bath? I'm much too big to bath in it now.'

'Well,' said Mummy, 'I thought maybe we would have a new baby to put in it soon.'

So Alison helped to wipe down the baby bath, and Mummy said, 'When the new baby comes, you will be my big girl, and help to bath the baby.'

Now the next day Alison came downstairs to see what Mummy was doing. She wasn't in the kitchen. She wasn't in the dining room. She wasn't hanging out the washing. Then Alison found her. She was looking in the chest of drawers to find Alison's old nappies.

'What are you doing, Mummy?' asked Alison.

'I'm looking for your old nappies,' said Mummy.

'Yes,' said Alison. 'But *why* are you looking for my old nappies? I'm much too big for nappies now.'

'Well,' said Mummy, 'I thought maybe we

would have a new baby to put nappies on soon.'

So Alison helped to find the nappies, and Mummy said, 'When the new baby comes, you will be my big girl and help to do the work. There is such a lot of work with new babies. You and I will manage together.'

Now the next day Alison came downstairs to see what Mummy was doing. She wasn't in the kitchen. She wasn't in the dining room. She wasn't outside hanging out the washing. Then Alison found her. She was by the front door with Daddy, putting on her coat.

'What are you doing, Mummy?' asked Alison.

'I think I will go to the hospital today,' said Mummy. 'It's time I had that new baby.'

So Alison and Daddy took Mummy to the hospital. Then Alison and Daddy came home and cooked the dinner, and washed up, and went to bed, all by themselves. They looked after each other beautifully till it was time for Mummy to bring the new baby home.

The baby was very small and very sweet. Its tiny hands and tiny fingernails could hold tightly to Alison's finger. Most of the time the baby screwed its eyes up tight and slept, but sometimes it got red in the face, and cried for milk and cuddling. It was hard work, looking after it. Everything happened just as Mummy said it would. They bathed the baby every day, and they put nappies on the baby every day, and they pushed the pram every day. And every day Alison helped, because she was a big girl.

Do you know another nice thing? When Mummy and the baby came home from hospital, they brought a lovely present for Alison. It was a red telephone, and Alison was delighted with it. I'd like a red telephone, wouldn't you?

The treat

Edna Williams

Are you sitting comfortably? Then I'll begin.

'If you are good,' said Mrs Rabbit to her five children, 'You shall have a treat.'

'Hurrah,' shouted the little rabbits, as they dashed off to be good somewhere.

The smallest rabbit stayed beside his mother. He was wondering what a 'treat' was like.

'Out of my way,' said Mrs Rabbit, as she lifted a pile of dirty dishes from the table and put them into a bowl of soapy water to be washed.

'Can I have a treat?' asked the smallest rabbit.

'A treat?' cried Mrs Rabbit, forgetting for the moment what she had promised. 'A treat! Your whole life is one great treat, if you ask me.' She swished the dishes about in the soapy water.

The smallest rabbit could tell that he was going to get no treat from his busy mother, whatever it was like. He wandered into the garden, where he saw a blackbird splashing about in a pool of water.

'Do you know what a treat is like, Blackbird?' he asked.

The blackbird flew up into a tree and sang a song:

> 'See me splashing, Oh, what fun,
> Water sparkling in the sun.
> See my feathers smooth and neat,
> Bath-time is a special *treat*.'

'So that's it,' thought the smallest rabbit. He jumped into the pool and splashed about until his fur was all wet and muddy. It was fun.

'I don't call that being good,' said Mrs Rabbit, as she rubbed him dry with a rough towel. 'Now, be off with you.'

'If that is a treat,' thought the smallest rabbit, 'I don't much like it.'

He wandered further into the garden and stopped in front of a big red poppy. 'Do you know what a treat is like, Poppy?' asked the smallest rabbit.

The Poppy nodded its head and sang quietly to itself:

> 'See my petals bright and red,
> See my nodding poppy head,
> All the winter, fast asleep,
> This is such a perfect *treat*.'

'So that's it,' thought the smallest rabbit. He stood beside the poppy and nodded his head. He nodded until his neck felt stiff and tired. 'If that is a treat,' thought the smallest rabbit, 'I don't much like it.'

'Come along,' called Mrs Rabbit. 'You have all been good; we shall have our treat.'

Mrs Rabbit spread a large rug on the grass and told the five little rabbits to sit themselves down. 'On such a lovely day, we are going to have a picnic,' she said.

The little rabbits ate bran sandwiches and drank carrot wine through freshly gathered straws.

'How delicious,' thought the smallest rabbit, as he munched his way through his tenth sandwich. He thought of the blackbird, happy with his splashing. He thought of the poppy, happy with its nodding. He watched his mother and the little rabbits, happily chewing.

'A treat is anything that makes you happy,' he told himself.

He was right.

Smarticats

Anne Wellington

Are you sitting comfortably? Then I'll begin.

Smarticat had ginger fur and long white whiskers. Smarticat had big ideas. He liked to be important. He stalked about the farmyard shouting, 'Yo ho ho! I'm a bold bad pirate. Yo ho ho!'

Mrs Nobb the farmer's wife said, 'Don't be ridiculous. You look like a silly old pussy cat to me.'

Smarticat looked at his reflection in the pond, and imagined himself in pirate's clothes. Shiny black boots, baggy green trousers, a red stripey jersey, and a black patch covering one eye. And sitting on his shoulder, a parrot!

'Those are the things I must get,' said Smarticat. 'Then I'll be a pirate. Yo ho ho!'

Smarticat caught a bee and put it into a bag. Then he said, 'The first thing I want is shiny boots. Duck wears shiny boots. Yo ho ho!'

Duck was in the farmyard, splashing in a puddle.

Smarticat shouted, 'I want your shiny boots.

> I'm a bold bad pirate
> With a nasty stinging bee;
> I'll let it out to sting you
> If you don't obey me.'

Duck heard the stinging bee buzzing in the bag. So she had to give her shiny boots to Smarticat. 'My poor little feet will get wet,' she said.

Smarticat said, 'Who cares? Now I want some trousers. Scarecrow wears trousers. Yo ho ho!'

Scarecrow was flapping at the birds in the cabbage field.

Smarticat shouted, 'I want your baggy trousers.

> I'm a bold bad pirate
> With a nasty stinging bee;
> I'll let it out to sting you
> If you don't obey me.'

Scarecrow heard the stinging bee buzzing in the bag. So he had to give his trousers to Smarticat. 'My poor stick legs will get cold,' he said.

Smarticat said, 'Rubbish! Now I want a jersey. Pig wears a jersey. Yo ho ho!'

Pig was in the pigsty eating a potato.

Smarticat shouted, 'I want your stripey jersey.

> I'm a bold bad pirate
> With a nasty stinging bee;
> I'll let it out to sting you
> If you don't obey me.'

Pig heard the stinging bee buzzing in the bag. So he had to give his jersey to Smarticat. 'My poor little tummy will get chilly,' he said.

Smarticat said, 'Fiddlesticks! Now I want a black patch. Owl wears a black patch. Yo ho ho!'

Owl was in the oak tree, with both eyes closed.

Smarticat shouted, 'I want your black patch.

> I'm a bold bad pirate
> With a nasty stinging bee;
> I'll let it out to sting you
> If you don't obey me.'

Owl heard the stinging bee buzzing in the bag. So he had to give his black patch to Smarticat. 'My poor little eye can't sleep,' he said.

Smarticat said, 'Nonsense! Now I want a parrot. Mrs Nobb has a parrot. Yo ho ho!'

Smarticat went in to the farmhouse kitchen. Mrs Nobb the farmer's wife was making scones for tea, and the fat green parrot was asleep in his cage.

Smarticat shouted, "I want your fat green parrot.

I'm a bold bad pirate
With a nasty stinging bee;
I'll let it out to sting you
If you don't obey me.'

Mrs Nobb the farmer's wife said, 'Don't be ridiculous. You look like a silly old pussy cat to me. But I'll let you have my parrot if you'll let me have your bee.' Smarticat undid the cage and let the parrot out. 'Now put your bee in the cage,' said Mrs Nobb. Smarticat had big ideas, but very little brain. He didn't understand that the cage could keep a parrot in, but not a little bee that could fly between the bars.

He heard the nasty bee buzzing in the bag. 'But you needn't think you'll sting me,' he said. 'Oh no! You're going straight in your cage, little bee. Like that!'

The poor little stinging bee was very, very angry. It flew around the parrot cage twice to get its speed up. Then out it buzzed, between the bars, straight towards Smarticat. Smarticat ran faster than he'd ever run before. Into the farmyard with the stinging bee behind him!

'Help!' shouted Smarticat. 'The bee will sting my tail!'

But Duck and Scarecrow and Pig and Owl said, 'Fiddlesticks and piffle! We don't care!'

The bee chased Smarticat twice around the

farmyard till his boots fell off. And Duck put them on.

The bee chased Smarticat twice around the farmyard till his trousers fell off. And Scarecrow put them on.

The bee chased Smarticat twice around the farmyard till his jersey fell off. And Pig put it on.

The bee chased Smarticat twice around the farmyard till his patch fell off. And Owl put it on.

Then the bee chased Smarticat twice around the farmyard and out and away till they disappeared from sight.

Smarticat came back next day looking very glum. When anyone asked him if the bee had caught him up, he pretended not to hear, and looked the other way. But he did have a bandage round his tail!

The lippity loppity
rabbit with the empty basket

Judith Drazin

Are you sitting comfortably? Then I'll begin.

Once upon a time, on a farm by a hill, there lived a Lippity Loppity Rabbit with an empty basket.

'Now what shall I put in my basket on this fine day?' said the rabbit to himself, and off he went, lippity loppity, to find the farmer's wife. The farmer's wife was working in the kitchen. She was rolling out the pastry to make a cheese pie for dinner.

'Please may I have something to put in my basket?' asked the rabbit, most politely.

'Certainly you may,' said the farmer's wife

kindly. 'Here is a piece of cheese and a loaf of good brown bread.'

So the rabbit put the cheese and the bread into his basket and off he went, lippity loppity, to find the farmer. The farmer was working hard in his garden, watering all his vegetables from a big can.

'Please may I have something to put in my basket?' asked the rabbit, most politely.

'Certainly you may,' said the farmer kindly. 'Here are three fresh carrots and a bunch of red radishes.'

So the rabbit put the carrots and the bunch of radishes in his basket and off he went, lippity loppity, until he came to the cherry tree. The cherry tree was in the orchard, waving her branches to and fro in the breeze.

'Please, Mrs Cherry Tree,' said the rabbit, most politely, 'may I have something to put in my basket?'

'Certainly you may,' said the cherry tree kindly. 'Here are four juicy cherries from my topmost branch.' The cherry tree shook her branches until the cherries fell to the ground, and the rabbit picked them up and put them in his basket. Then off he went, lippity loppity once more until he came to the beehive that stood by the lavender bush. The bees were making honey for their winter store.

'Please,' said the rabbit, most politely, when he saw them, 'please may I have something to put in my basket?'

'Certainly you mmmmmmay,' said the bees very kindly. 'Here is a honeycomb for you, dripping with rich honey.'

But when the Lippity Loppity Rabbit put the honeycomb carefully in his basket he had a big surprise. His basket was quite full up. 'My goodness,' he said to himself. 'I think it is time to climb to the meadow on the side of the hill and have a picnic.' So the Lippity Loppity Rabbit took his basket and climbed and climbed, nearly to the top of the hill, until he reached the meadow where the buttercups grew. Then out of his basket he took:

a piece of cheese
a loaf of brown bread
three fresh carrots
a bunch of radishes
four cherries from the topmost branch of the cherry tree
and a golden honeycomb dripping with honey.

Soon the basket was quite empty again, but the Lippity Loppity Rabbit was as full as full. 'That was the nicest picnic I have ever had,' he said to himself as he licked his sticky paws. Then he gave a great big yawn and, curling himself up in the sunshine, he fell fast asleep.

Gilbert the ostrich

Jane Holiday

Are you sitting comfortably? Then I'll begin.

The Dancer family lived in an ordinary house. Mr Dancer was ordinary. Mrs Dancer was ordinary. Martin and Donna were ordinary children. And Conker was an ordinary dog – black and white with a wagging tail. So how did they come to have an *ostrich* living with them? Nobody knew.

Anyway, the ostrich *was* living there and his name was Gilbert. Gilbert was a handsome bird with a small head, a fluffy body, long legs and big, brown eyes. He was so tall he could change all the light bulbs in the house without standing on a chair *but* he dropped them SMASH on the floor.

Everyone said what a lovely bird Gilbert was, but he had some nasty habits. He ate nuts and bolts. He ate jam jar lids. He ate the bathroom plug. He ate thirty pence left on the kitchen table. He ate the top of Donna's fountain-pen. She could still write with it, so she didn't mind. He ate the laces of Martin's football boots. Martin *did* mind. He shouted at Gilbert, 'You're a nasty, greedy bird!'

Gilbert was sad. He didn't know it was wrong to eat bootlaces.

In some ways Gilbert was very good. He drank all his milk up. Every morning, Mrs Dancer said, 'Drink all your milk, Martin,' and 'Drink your milk, Donna.' Martin and Donna always said, 'Ugh!' but Gilbert had finished every drop.

He could run very fast too. So Mrs Dancer sent him to the shops. He carried the shopping-basket on his wing. In the basket was the shopping-list and some money. Sometimes, too, he helped clean the house. He could reach up to the ceiling and dust the cobwebs away.

Everyone liked Gilbert. He was such a *polite* bird.

One afternoon Mr and Mrs Dancer took Martin and Donna to the cinema. They left Gilbert at home. Last time he went he had eaten two ashtrays. Now there was a big notice outside the cinema. It read: NO OSTRICHES.

Mrs Dancer was worried about leaving Gilbert. 'I hope he doesn't feel hungry.'

Mr Dancer was worried too. 'I hope he doesn't feel lonely.'

Martin and Donna were glad he wasn't coming. They always had to sit in the back row when Gilbert came, because he was so tall.

'Be a good bird, Gilbert,' said Mrs Dancer. She left him a pint of milk and some cheese. Mr Dancer left him an old screwdriver. Martin and Donna left him some marbles.

When they came home at six o'clock, Gilbert was fast asleep in an armchair.

'He's drunk the milk,' said Mrs Dancer.

'He's eaten the cheese,' said Mr Dancer, 'and half the screwdriver.'

'And all the marbles,' said Martin and Donna.

Those weren't the only things Gilbert had eaten.

'I can't get into the bathroom,' called Martin.

'We can't get into the bedrooms,' called Mrs Dancer and Donna.

Do you know *why* they couldn't? Gilbert had eaten *all* the doorknobs. He hadn't left a single one anywhere. He'd even eaten the knob on the oven door. Mr Dancer managed to open one door with some tools. Then he opened the other doors.

They didn't have new door knobs put on though. Now all the doors in the Dancers' house are *swing* doors. You *push* them open. They *swing* to behind you. Everyone liked them better, and said that Gilbert was a good bird really.

I wonder what he will eat next. Do you?

The dragon of Penhesgyn
A traditional story
Moira Miller

Listen 'ere now and I'll tell you a story.

There was once a very fine lord and lady lived in a castle – and there was no finer castle in all of Wales. It stood at the bottom of a high mountain with a little village around it. And at the top of the mountain, in a cave, there lived a great, ugly dragon.

Now it happened one day that the fine lord and lady had a little baby son called Hugh. Oh, a fine baby he was. And nothing would do but they had to have a christening party, and invite everyone who was anyone to come to it including an old Welsh Wizard who was a sort of great uncle of the fine lady's.

The old wizard arrived late, all flustered and flummoxed, and went in to look at the baby.

'Dew!' he said. 'It's a fine little lad you have there. Pity about the dragon.'

'Dragon? What dragon?' asked the father.

'Big one up the mountain,' said the wizard. 'When your son's fifteen the dragon'll come down and eat him. There's horrible for you!'

'Impossible!' said the father.

'Oh, I'm not often wrong about these things, bach,' said the wizard. 'Part of my job, you know.'

And before they could ask him any more questions about the dragon, the wizard vanished in a puff of smoke.

But gradually they forgot what the wizard had said, and the years passed. Hugh grew up to be a fine little boy, and his very best friend was a boy from the village called David. His father was Jones the Smith, and he'd been born on the same day at exactly the same time as Hugh, to the very minute. So you see of course they were the best of friends. They did everything together. Played in the fields, climbed trees, fished in the river, and sometimes they climbed the mountain. But not too high, mind, because of the dragon at the top of course. And so the boys went on, playing and laughing together, until they were nearly fifteen.

On the day before his birthday Hugh's father called him in.

'I'm afraid the time has come for you to leave us, boyo,' he said. 'If you stay here much longer this terrible dragon will come looking, and who knows what'll happen? You're going for a long holiday to your Auntie Gwyneth in England. There isn't a Welsh dragon in the world would follow you there.' Before he knew properly what was happening Hugh was bundled off to Auntie Gwyneth in England.

Well, this was a sad state of affairs, and David was very upset about losing his best friend. And the more he thought about it the more angry he became. He was like that, do you see.

'Only a dragon it is,' he said, 'and dragons can be killed. I'll have a go at this one myself.'

He set off and climbed up the mountain, higher and higher. Farther than he or Hugh had ever been before. Up to where the dragon slept in his huge dark cave.

David scrambled up over the stones and boulders and at last he heard a great roaring sound. He crept up and peered round the corner of a rock, then nearly fell over with surprise. There was a great green dragon, lying sleeping in the sun, snoring and roaring something horrible. He was as big as a railway engine, I can tell you.

'Dew! It's horrible he is,' whispered David to himself. 'He'll take some killing. I'll have to think about this!'

He hurried back down the mountain again, and thought about it. He thought for days and days. And then – oh – he had a very clever idea. Listen, I'll tell you about it.

First of all he went to the castle kitchen and borrowed the biggest copper frying pan he could find. He took it home and started to polish it. He rubbed and rubbed. His father, Jones the Smith, rubbed and rubbed. His mam, Mrs Jones the Smith, rubbed and rubbed. Even the baby had a go. And at last that copper pan was just like a mirror. You could see your face in it, clear as clear.

Then David took his pan and climbed back up the mountain with it. He put it down carefully, and started to dig a great big hole, right in front of the dragon's cave. He waited till the dragon was asleep, mind; he wasn't daft, our David. And when that hole was dug, he put the pan in the bottom of it. Then he got all the people from the village to come up and watch what happened next.

He stood himself on the other side of the hole from the dragon and hurled a stone across at it.

'It's an idle great thing you are!' he shouted. 'Waken up, you horrible monster.'

The dragon turned over and grunted in his sleep, breathing out flames and smoke, and scorching all the grass around him.

David threw another rock. A bigger one this time.

'Call yourself a dragon, man!' he yelled. 'You're useless. Couldn't scare a mouse.'

The dragon woke up, thoroughly angry by this time, and roared a roar that was heard in every valley clear down to Aberystwyth. The great beast stood up and shook himself all over, and, boys, he was a *horrible* sight to behold. He roared another terrible roar and started towards David. But then he stopped at the edge of the hole.

He looked down, and there at his feet staring up at him was – what do you think? Another horrible dragon. Well that really put him out, I can tell you.

He leapt into that hole howling and roaring, and do you know, the dragon in the hole was not in the least bit frightened of him. It roared back, just as loud and just as ugly. Well that started the fight. David and the village people stood and stared. Fair amazed they were at the goings on. The roaring and howling and clouds of smoke and fire and whatnot. That dragon was going fit to bust, fighting with his own reflection in an old copper frying pan. Dragons are big, look you, but they're not very bright.

Well, at last it was all over. The stupid beast had fair exhausted himself, and the great clouds of smoke were just a little tiny trickle. Then David borrowed a sword and jumped down into the hole. One swipe and he'd chopped off the dragon's head. Clean as a whistle.

The people from the village were overjoyed.

'Alleluia!' they shouted, dancing back down the mountain. 'Our David's a Hero. The dragon's dead.'

So Hugh came back home again from his Auntie Gwyneth's, and he and David went fishing again, and even climbed to the very top of the mountain. They were the very best of friends all their lives after that.

And what about the Welsh Wizard? Well, I'll tell you one thing, nobody ever asked *him* to a christening again!

Angela and the custard pump

Jan Dean

Are you sitting comfortably? Then I'll begin.

Angela was cross.

She stamped her feet and made bad-tempered noises.

She marched up and down, snorting and grumbling. Oh yes, Angela was very cross.

The sun was shining and Angela wanted to be outside with it. She wanted to go to the park and throw bread to the ducks. She wanted to go to the park and play in the sand. She wanted to go to the park and whoosh down the slide.

But no, she couldn't feed the ducks, no, she couldn't make sand pies. No, she couldn't whoosh and thump. She had to stay inside and watch the custard pump!

Angela's grandmother had a shop. She made cakes and bread and biscuits. Everyone Angela knew came into grandma's shop, and they all said that Angela's grandma's cakes and bread and biscuits were the most wonderful and delicious that they had ever tasted. But there was nothing, they said, nothing, nothing, nothing at all more marvellous and melting than Angela's grandma's creamy custard cupcakes. And they were right.

Some people said that Angela's grandma's creamy custard cupcakes were so amazingly mouthwatering that they must be magic. And they were right too. In the back of grandma's shop gleamed a strange machine. A fat shiny drum churned round and round, and a long silver tube stuck out into a bowl. Out of the tube and into the bowl poured the custard, a beautiful sweet stream of marvellous, magical custard.

Angela was not impressed. She didn't want to look after the pump – and she told it so. She hated the pump – and she told it so. The pump said nothing but, "Splinkety glug. Splinkety glug glug glug glug. Splinkety glug. Splinkety glug. Splinkety glug glug glug.' Which is what it always said.

Angela was so cross that she almost exploded. She raised both arms and shook both fists and her face grew redder and redder. She jumped into the air and began to shout. She howled and screeched and screamed and yelled and called the custard pump all the names she could think of!

Suddenly everything went quiet. Angela did not shout and the pump did not go, 'Splinkety glug.' Instead a huge splodge of custard squirted through the air and sprayed all over the wall. A great fat bubble of custard hiccuped from the tube and blubbered onto the floor, and an enormous bomb of custard burst from the drum and splattered all over the ceiling. Angela stood very still.

Angela's grandma came in carrying a red umbrella. She looked round the room and she looked at Angela. Angela looked at the floor. Custard dripped from the ceiling. Angela began to feel very sticky.

Angela's grandma looked at Angela for a very long time. Then she said, 'This looks like a job for the custard fairy to me. Pass me the 'phone book.'

So Angela handed her grandmother the 'phone book, and her grandmother looked under F for fairy. Then she went away to make the 'phone call.

While Angela waited for the custard fairy to arrive she began to clean up the room. She was halfway through mopping the floor when he appeared. He was a small man in blue overalls, and he popped out of the air carrying a large tool bag. On the back of his overalls MAGIC MACHINE MAINTENANCE MECHANIC was printed in glittering gold letters.

'What's this 'ere, then?' he said as he began to

fish around inside the broken pump. 'There's something very nasty in 'ere,' and out of the machine he pulled a black tangled lump.

'Well, no wonder it blew up!' he said.

'What is it?' asked Angela.

'The one thing guaranteed to stop a magic pump. Bad temper. A very large, a very ugly, very nasty piece of bad temper!'

Then he patted the pump and it set off again quite happily. 'Splinkety glug. Splinkety glug. Splinkety glug glug glug,' it went. 'Splinkety glug. Splinkety glug. Splinkety glug glug glug.'

'Shall I take this with me, or do you want it back?' He held the black lump out to Angela.

'No, you take it,' Angela said. 'I feel better without it.'

'Righto, then,' smiled the maintenance fairy, 'I'll be off down the road. Seems there's a pump down there running lumpy.' And he disappeared with a sort of 'ping'.

'I'm sorry, custard pump,' said Angela. 'I do like you really.'

'Splinkety glug,' said the pump. 'Splinkety glug. Splinkety glug glug glug,' and blew her a big custardy kiss.

Amy Kate's lion

Joyce Williams

Are you sitting comfortably? Then I'll begin.

It was a windy day. Amy Kate was looking for a lion. She marched along the street with a butterfly net over her shoulder, and her friends all asked, 'How are you going to catch him, Amy Kate?'

'With my butterfly net,' Amy Kate replied. 'That's what it's for.'

'What will you do with him when you've got him?'

'I shall take him to the zoo,' said Amy Kate. 'That's where all the lions belong.'

'Won't he be very fierce and frighten everyone?' they asked.

'I shall talk to him gently while I tie a bit of string to his collar – then he'll be quite tame,' Amy Kate assured them. 'There's no need for anyone to be frightened.'

'*I'm* frightened!' said the littlest child, but nobody heard her.

All her friends got into a long line behind Amy Kate and followed her along the street. 'Amy Kate's looking for a lion!' they told all the people. 'And we're helping her!'

'*I'm* not!' said the littlest child.

On and on they went. The wind smacked their cheeks and tugged their hair and snatched all their breaths away. Amy Kate's friends began to get tired. 'Where's this lion, Amy Kate?' they said. 'We don't believe there *is* one after all.'

'Yes, there is,' said Amy Kate. And just then a Big Brown Something came rushing out of nowhere along the street towards them. 'Here he comes!' cried Amy Kate. 'Don't be frightened!'

But the children *were* frightened. They scrambled over the wall into old Mrs Toppett's garden.

'Mrs Toppett, Mrs Toppett, there's a lion in the road and Amy Kate is chasing him!' they shouted.

The old lady came out of her cottage. 'Dear me! A lion! Has it escaped from the zoo?' Then she saw the Big Brown Something rushing along with Amy Kate after it.

Mr Podger came out of his house next door. Mrs Toppett called to him, 'Oh, Mr Podger! A lion has escaped from the zoo and Amy Kate is chasing him!'

'Goodness me!' said Mr Podger. He put on his spectacles and peered along the road. He saw a Big Brown Something going very fast, and Amy Kate racing after it, brandishing her butterfly net. Suddenly they both turned a corner and disappeared.

Policeman Blackie came by. Mr Podger, Mrs Toppett and all the children clustered round him. 'Policeman Blackie!' they shouted all together. 'A lion has escaped from the zoo and Amy Kate has chased it around a corner!'

'Hmm,' said the policeman. 'This calls for an investigation.' He strode off down the street with big heavy steps. Mr Podger trotted after him. Mrs Toppett hurried after Mr Podger. Behind her came all the children in a straggly line, the littlest child last of all clinging to her brother.

At the corner Policeman Blackie stopped, and Mr Podger, Mrs Toppett and all the children bumped into one another as they stopped too. They peeped around the corner. There, partly hidden behind a dustbin, was the Big Brown Something, but Amy Kate was nowhere to be seen.

'The lion must have eaten her!' the littlest child whispered.

Suddenly the Big Brown Something sprang out at them from behind the dustbin, and everybody screamed.

'Why, it's only a large paper bag after all!' said Policeman Blackie. 'The wind must have blown it along.' He began to laugh.

'Just fancy that!' declared Mrs Toppett and Mr Podger. 'A brown paper bag!' They went off home looking rather disappointed.

'But where is Amy Kate?' demanded all the children.

Just then Amy Kate bobbed up from behind the dustbin, and began to whistle in an offhand manner. She shouldered her butterfly net and strolled towards them.

'Amy Kate, Amy Kate, where's the lion?' chanted the children.

'Gone,' said Amy Kate.

'Back to the zoo?'

Amy Kate shook her head. 'He begged me not to send him to the zoo. He said his home was in Africa, so I made him promise to go there straight away. And that's what he did.'

'What are you doing now, Amy Kate?' they asked.

'Me? I'm looking for an elephant,' replied

Amy Kate. 'Want to come along?'

'Will he bite?' asked the littlest child.

'Of course not,' said Amy Kate. 'He'll give us rides on his back.'

'Hurrah!' cried all the children. 'We're looking for an elephant!' They got into a line behind Amy Kate. Then they all went whistling down the street.

All it needs is a wash

Armorel Kay Walling

Are you sitting comfortably? Then I'll begin.

Tina went to a jumble sale with her Mum – and bought a hat. Not a hat for herself, not a hat for her doll, but a hat for her big brother Bob.

Bob was at a football match. Bob loved watching football. He always wore something blue and white when he went to a football match because those were the colours of his favourite team. The hat Tina bought was blue and white, too: blue and white stripes with a big blue bobble on top.

'Bob can wear it to football,' said Tina, 'to keep his ears warm.'

'It's grubby,' said Mum.

'It's beautiful,' said the jumble sale lady. 'All it needs is a wash.'

So as soon as she got home, Tina washed the hat. She stood on a chair at the sink and shook soap powder into the bowl. She turned on the taps and woggled the water in the bowl until it was dancing with bubbles. Then she turned them off again and began to scrub. She rubbed and scrubbed. She scrubbed and rubbed for so long that her hands became all crinkly from being in the water, and she used most of the soap powder. But the hat – why the hat came out as clean as new!

'There!' said Tina. 'I *knew* all it needed was a wash!'

She went outside, let down the line, and pegged the hat out to dry.

Then she sat down with Mum for a drink and a biscuit. (It was a chocolate biscuit – rather sticky.) After a while, she thought, 'I wonder if that hat's dry yet?' and went to look.

It wasn't, of course, so she decided to help *blow* it dry. She stood very close and pursed her lips and went 'Foooo!' Sadly, she still had chocolate on her lips, and when she went 'Fooo!' some of it came off and left a smudge on the hat.

'Never mind,' thought Tina, 'it's only a little smudge,' and she went indoors to paint pictures.

But after a while she thought, 'I wonder if it's dry *now*,' and went to look.

It wasn't, of course, so she tried to *squeeeeeze* it dry. Sadly, her hands were still pink from painting, and when she squeezed some of the pink came off on the hat and made a stain.

'Never mind,' thought Tina, 'it's only a little

stain,' and she went to watch television.

But after a while, she thought, 'I wonder if it's dry *yet*,' and went to have another look. It *still* wasn't, so very carefully she took the hat off the line and laid it on her swing. She decided to push it high into the sky so that the winter sun could dry it. Sadly, the hat flew off and fell – right into the cabbages. They left a muddy streak.

'Oh dear,' thought Tina. 'It's quite a big streak.'

Suddenly, she heard Bob coming home from football. She didn't want him to see the hat – not until it was dry – so she ran indoors and pushed it quickly down behind the radiator. And then, what with Bob being excited because his favourite team had won, and there being apple crumble for supper, Tina forgot about the hat – until next day.

How proud she was when she remembered that she'd washed it all by herself. She pulled it out from behind the radiator. It was rather dusty, and it *did* still have a chocolate smudge and a pink paint stain and a muddy cabbage streak but – now it was *dry*.

She gave it to Bob.

'What's this?' he asked gruffly.

'A present for you. I bought it with my own money – to keep your ears warm at football.'

Bob looked at the hat slowly; at the chocolate

smudge and the pink paint stain and the muddy streak and the dusty patch, and for a moment Tina thought he didn't like it.

Then he smiled. 'Thank you,' he said. 'Thank you, Tina. It's a beautiful hat and it *will* keep my ears warm at football. There's just one thing... it's grubby.'

'Oh *that*,' said Tina. 'Don't worry about *that*. All it needs is a wash!' And off she skipped to get the soap powder again.

ANIMAL TALES FROM
LISTEN WITH MOTHER

ANIMAL TALES FROM

LISTEN
WITH MOTHER

With an introduction by
Jean Rogers

Illustrated by Douglas Hall

Contents

Introduction   7
Green grobblop   9
   Eugenie Summerfield
The adventures of
Young Hedgehog and Mole   14
   Vera Rushbrooke
Little Pig and the hot dry summer   19
   Margaret Gore
The owl who didn't give a hoot   23
   Irene Holness
Frizby's royal invitation   28
   Val Annan
The little cat with the very long tail   33
   Diana Webb
Chick, Chicklet and Chick-a-Ling   37
   Ivy Eastwick
Little fly on the ceiling   43
   Angela Pickering
Hugo the hippo sings   47
   Rachel Ford

The dustbin cat 51
  May K. Randell
Mr Herbert Herbert's holiday 55
  Margery Goulden
Wriggly Worm and the new pet 59
  Eugenie Summerfield
Nozzle the ant-eater 64
  Christopher Newby
The warthog and the unicorn 68
  Sandra Hannaford
Just a bad day 74
  Rosalie Eisenstein
The secret 77
  Kathleen Pateman
Ary the spider 81
  Irene Holness
Basil Brown, the fat cat 86
  Richard Coughlin
The sheep who didn't count 93
  Irene Holness

Introduction

My children grew up with 'Listen with Mother'. At about the time I joined the programme in the early seventies, Jeremy, my eldest child, was two. He always enjoyed being read to. When he was only a year old he would sit on my lap and encourage me to make up stories about the pictures he saw in his nursery rhyme book.

When I started reading stories for 'Listen with Mother', I would invariably pretend I was in my dining room – not sitting in front of a microphone in the studio – and that I was telling the stories to Jeremy, and only to Jeremy. It is a very personal activity, story-telling, and I am sure it only comes across on radio if it is approached on a one to one basis. The dining room had a bright yellow floor and I'm certain that's why all my precious memories of the programme are bathed in sunshine!

Telling stories to children encourages their imaginations and their understanding and use of words. It certainly worked in Jeremy's case. By the time he went to 'big school', although he was still unable to read, his teacher – a lovely lady called Mrs Lowrie whom my son adored! – would sit him in front of the class where, she said, he would tell the other children the most wonderful stories all by himself.

It is such a special, magical experience cuddling a little one to you and sharing a good story such as the ones you will find in this book. Children especially like stories about animals. Tell them it's about a cat, or a tortoise, or a singing hippopotamus, and just see their eyes light up. I sometimes wish Justine, my youngest child, was not past the stage of sitting on my lap, but she is twelve now.

However, the television character I play at the moment, in a series set on a farm, runs the local playgroup, so I still get opportunities to tell exciting stories to little ones; stories like 'The Owl Who Didn't Give a Hoot' and 'Frizby's Royal Invitation' (I still have a soft spot for stories with princesses in them) and say those nostalgic words: 'Are you sitting comfortably?' You are? Well, I'll begin.

Jean Rogers

Green grobblop

Eugenie Summerfield

Are you sitting comfortably? Then I'll begin.

At first nobody knew what the green grobblop was or even where it came from. Ben found it on the doorstep one Monday morning. He came running in from the garden calling to his mother.

'Come and see! There's a funny green hairy thing out here. It's ever so small and ever so sad. Can I play with it?'

Ben's Mum, who was in the kitchen doing the washing, came to have a look.

'I don't know what it is,' she said, 'and it doesn't look very clean. I think I'd better give it a good wash before you play with it.'

She always washed everything on a Monday. So she washed it. She was going to peg it up to dry when she heard it say, 'Don't peg me up on the clothes line. A green grobblop like me should be put in a nice warm room.'

Ben's Mum was so surprised to hear the grobblop speak, she said, 'Oh, I'm sorry!' and asked, 'What did you say your name was?'

'I'm a green grobblop,' it said, and it did look so small and sad. Ben's Mum was a kind lady. She took it at once and put it on the curly cuddly rug in the sitting room.

'That's much better,' said the grobblop, nodding its small green head. 'Now I should like tea and chocolate biscuits and some bananas.'

'There is only one banana,' said Ben, who was looking forward to eating it for his tea.

'Well, that will have to do for now then,' sighed the grobblop, looking smaller and sadder than ever. 'But in future, I would like three for my tea.'

After he had eaten the banana, the grobblop had four helpings of biscuits. He was just drinking his fifth cup of tea when Ben's Dad came home from work.

'What's that?' asked Ben's Dad. When Ben

and his Mum told him, Ben's Dad had to agree that the grobblop did look small and sad.

'And it will need to be well looked after,' he said.

All the rest of the week the grobblop sat on the curly cuddly rug. Ben's Mum fed him and Ben played with him whenever he wanted. At the end of the week Ben's Mum said: 'I'm afraid I shall need some more money now that we have a grobblop to feed. It does eat rather a lot.'

'I can see that,' said Ben's Dad, and he looked worried. He wasn't at all sure that his boss would pay him more money just because he now had a green grobblop to feed.

'Perhaps,' he said, 'when the green grobblop gets bigger and stronger, he'll be able to do some useful jobs about the house.'

'I hope so,' agreed Ben's Mum. She had been doing everything for the grobblop, giving him the biggest helpings, letting him have the most comfortable place to sit in the sitting room and the warmest blankets on his bed.

'I can think of lots of useful things he could do,' said Ben's Mum.

No sooner was this said than the grobblop said, 'I'll have to go to bed. I'm not at all well.'

The doctor was called and he came almost at once. He wasn't used to treating grobblops, but he said, 'He does look green and small and sad!

He needs someone to look after him. He's to stay in bed a day or two and take this medicine to make him well and strong.'

The grobblop liked his medicine almost as much as he liked tea and biscuits and bananas. He liked staying in bed even better than he liked lying on the curly cuddly rug in the sitting room. So he stayed in bed and had all his meals brought up. All the time he was growing bigger and stronger, Ben's Mum grew thinner and more tired. Until one day, she said, 'I'm quite worn out.' Ben's Dad sent her to bed and called the doctor who said, 'You're to stay in bed a day or two and let someone look after you.'

The grobblop heard what the doctor said. He peeped in to see Ben's Mum. 'She does look so sad and small,' thought the grobblop who was now big and strong. He felt ashamed. He went downstairs at once.

He cleaned the kitchen, dusted the rooms, and made a delicious meal which he took up to her on a tray. He did this every day until Ben's Mum was well again. Then he said to her, 'I've come to say it's time I went away.'

'You don't have to go,' said Ben's Mum. 'You really can stay as long as you like.'

But the grobblop replied, 'No, I'm big enough and strong enough to look after myself now. I won't forget how well you looked after me and I'll write to you sometimes.'

Ben and his Mum and Dad were quite sorry to say goodbye to the grobblop. He went to live at the seaside and he did write to them. He sent them some lovely picture postcards and he's asked them all to come and stay with him for their next summer holiday.

The adventures of Young Hedgehog and Mole

Vera Rushbrooke

Are you sitting comfortably? Then I'll begin.

Young Hedgehog and Mole were sitting at the bottom of the oak tree in the hedge, chatting.

'I lead such a dull life!' said Young Hedgehog. 'It's the same old things every day! Get up, have something to eat, sit in the sun, have something else to eat, have a chat with Rabbit, go to bed, and that's all I ever do! I wish I had a more exciting life!'

'I never thought about it before,' said Mole, 'but now you come to mention it, I suppose it is

14

rather dull doing the same old things every day.'

'Well,' said Young Hedgehog, 'should we change it by going out to find adventures?'

Mole thought a bit.

'Very well,' he said, 'but not for long as I've just started on a new tunnel.'

So they shut their little doors and set off to find adventures.

'This is exciting!' said Young Hedgehog, trotting along. 'We'll go a new way neither of us has been before.' So they trotted along the strange path, laughing and whistling. Presently they came to what looked like a tunnel.

'This looks interesting!' said Young Hedgehog. 'Should we go down this tunnel and see what's at the other end?'

'Well,' said Mole, 'I'm always going down tunnels! But this one is so big!'

So they crept into the tunnel.

'It's very dark!' said Young Hedgehog.

'Tunnels always are!' said Mole.

Just then, ahead of them, came a swishing, sloshing and splashing of water. And before they could say, 'Dandelions!' down the tunnel came a stream of water and it washed Young Hedgehog and Mole out of the tunnel and into the daisy field. For it wasn't really a tunnel they'd gone into, but a water pipe coming from the farm and somebody had turned on the tap.

'Goodness me!' cried Mole, 'I wasn't expecting that!' and he shook the water off his velvet coat.

'Never mind,' said Young Hedgehog, pretending he didn't care about getting soaked with water. 'That's part of the fun, isn't it?'

'Is it?' said Mole.

Then Young Hedgehog laughed and then Mole laughed, and they told each other it was fun having adventures.

After they'd dried themselves they trotted on, picking up a tasty bit here and there to eat on the way. After a while, they came across a big old basket full of cabbage leaves. There was a hole in one side of it.

'Let's climb in there,' said Young Hedgehog, 'and see what's inside.'

'Isn't it exciting doing new things!' said Mole. 'It's quite a change from digging tunnels!'

Just as they had climbed inside, the basket began to move. Someone was carrying it. Young Hedgehog and Mole were not sure what to do.

'We're moving!' cried Mole.

'Yes,' said Young Hedgehog, 'I wonder where we are going!'

'I don't think I like it very much,' said Mole. 'I like to know where I'm going to.'

'Oh, but that's the fun of it!' said Young

Hedgehog. 'It's not an adventure if you know where you're going.'

'I suppose not,' said Mole.

'Then look happy!' Young Hedgehog said.

Just as he said that, the basket of cabbage leaves with Mole and Young Hedgehog was tipped out into a chicken run. When the hens saw Young Hedgehog and Mole in their chicken run there was a great squawking and cackling.

'Out! Out!' shrieked the hens. 'Hedgehogs and rats are not allowed in here!'

Mole was furious.

'I'm not a rat! I'm a mole!'

'Whatever you are, you're not allowed in here. Just hens and chickens. Out with you!'

Young Hedgehog and Mole squeezed under the wire as fast as they could and trotted off.

'It was really fun, wasn't it!' said Young Hedgehog.

'No!' cried Mole. 'It wasn't! And I want to go home! I've been soaked with water in a tunnel, chased by angry hens, and I've been called a rat! I've had enough, I'm going home!'

'All right,' said Young Hedgehog, who was really glad because he wanted to go home too. So off they went.

When they got home, Mole said, 'Thank goodness! Let me get inside and have a warm sleep!' And he dived down his tunnel and nobody saw him for days.

Young Hedgehog, feeling cold and tired, opened his little green door and banged it behind him.

'From now on I'm going to stay at home! There's nothing nicer than doing the ordinary things you do every day like sitting in the sun, and eating something nice, and chatting with Rabbit, and having a nice warm sleep.'

And from then on, nobody ever heard Young Hedgehog talking about adventures.

Little Pig and the hot dry summer

Margaret Gore

Are you sitting comfortably? Then I'll begin.

'I wish it would rain!' said Little Pig.

There had been no rain for weeks and weeks, and all the pigs were puffing and grunting with the heat. In the field beyond the pigsties the ground was as hard as an overbaked cake.

No rain meant that there was no mud. And what Little Pig loved most of all was mud. Thick, squelchy, oozy *mud*! Little Pig would roll on his back, waving his four pink trotters in the air and squealing with delight.

'If *only* it would rain!' sighed Little Pig. 'This

19

summer has been so hot and dry, and I *do* love a mucky roll in the mud!'

In the sty next door to Little Pig lived Big Pig. Big Pig was a terrible boaster.

'*I* could make it rain – if I *wanted* to, that is,' he said. None of the other pigs believed Big Pig. Especially Quick Pig, who had a sharp tongue.

Quick Pig said, 'Go on then, *make* it rain, Big Pig!'

'I – I don't think I have time just now,' replied Big Pig.

Slow Pig grunted, 'He knows he can't, that's why.'

Big Pig pretended to be busy rooting about for something to eat. Slow Pig had hardly moved all summer – except to eat. He just lay by the wall, snoring. Even Kind Pig, who was a most patient pig, grew tired of Slow Pig's snoring.

The weather grew hotter and hotter. And *still* no rain.

'I don't think I shall ever have a good, mucky roll in the mud again!' wept Little Pig.

'Of course you will, Little Pig,' said Kind Pig. 'I'm sure it must rain soon!'

And it *did* rain. That very night.

First came a few big spots. Splash, splash, splodge. Then it rained faster and faster, and heavier and heavier.

Now it was simply bucketing down! The rain

hissed on the roof; it swept across the yard; it gushed down the drains.

It made a noise like a hundred pigs all drinking at once from a high trough!

But the trouble was, now that the rain had started it wouldn't stop. It went on all the next day, and all the next night, and all the next day after that!

'It's never going to stop raining!' squealed Little Pig. Quick Pig blamed Big Pig.

'*You* made it rain – and now you can't stop it!'

'It's not *my* fault,' grumbled Big Pig.

There was water everywhere. Even the field became a lake. The ducks from the pond were able to swim right up to the wall of the pigsties. *Inside*, the pigs were huddled together, squealing; and *outside* the ducks swam up and down teasing them, and laughing their quacky laughs.

The water got higher and higher. Little Pig was frightened, but Kind Pig said, 'Don't cry, Little Pig. Look, here is someone coming to save us.'

It was Tom the farmhand. He came sailing across the field on a wooden raft which he had just knocked together from an old door.

Tom put down a plank from the pigsties on to the raft, and then the pigs walked across it. First Quick Pig – because he was always first with everything (especially eating!).

Then Big Pig, because he had knocked everyone else out of the way. Then Kind Pig, who showed Little Pig how to walk along the plank without falling off, and lastly Slow Pig – it *had* to be Slow Pig didn't it!

The pigs sailed away on their raft, to a dry place on the other side of the field. And there they had to stay, until, next morning, they were awakened by Little Pig squealing and squealing.

'Wake up, wake up,' cried Little Pig. 'The sun's shining, and all the water has gone! We can go home.'

Little Pig was quite right. They did go home, but not by raft, because there was no water left. They had to go by tractor, because the whole field was a mass of – MUD!

'Squelchy, oozy, delicious MUD!' cried Little Pig. When they reached home, the pigs trotted happily back into their own sties. First Quick Pig, then Big Pig, then Kind Pig, and last of all, Slow Pig.

But where was *Little* Pig?

The pigs crowded to the wall and looked over into the field.

There was Little Pig. He was lying on his back in the mud, waving his four pink trotters in the air and squealing with delight.

'I *do* love a good mucky roll!' said Little Pig.

The owl who didn't
give a hoot

Irene Holness

Are you sitting comfortably? Then I'll begin.

'Tu whit tu whoo!' hooted Mrs Owl. 'Come, children. Now you-oo!'

'Tu whit tu whoo!' chorused three of the little owls perched on a high branch of the old oak tree.

'Itty ooo!' chirruped the smallest owl. His brother and his sisters chuckled.

Mrs Owl didn't think it was at all funny. She looked sadly at the smallest owl.

'Oh, Drew,' she sighed. 'Why can't you learn to hoot properly like Hugh, Sue and Pru?'

Drew looked up at the bright silver moon and tried again.

'Itty ooo, itty ooo,' he sang. 'I'll never get it right!'

All that night Drew practised hooting, but still all he could manage was 'Itty ooo,' in a funny, squeaky voice. At last, as the sun rose, the deep blue night sky began to grow lighter.

'Bedtime, children,' Mrs Owl said, when they had eaten their supper.

Mrs Owl and three small owlets were soon sound asleep in their home in a hollow tree, but Drew was too worried to sleep.

'There must be someone, somewhere,' he thought, 'who can teach me how to hoot. I must go and see.'

So, in the soft, grey light of early morning, he left the nest and flew on his strong silent wings across the fields to the farmyard. There he saw the farm cat.

'Hello, cat,' called Drew. 'You have eyes which see in the dark like mine. Can you hoot?'

'Meiow, Naow!' grinned the cat.

So Drew peeped into the barn.

'Can you hoot?' he asked Daisy the cow.

'Mooo, noooo!' answered Daisy.

Gilly the Goose stalked across the farmyard.

'Good morning, Gilly,' cried Drew. 'Please, can you hoot?'

'Honk, honk! Bonk, honk! I should think not!' snapped Gilly haughtily.

Brag, the brown dog, sat outside the farmhouse door and howled, 'Ow-wow-wo-ow.'

'That's a fine song,' exclaimed Drew. 'Can you hoot, Brag?'

'No,' growled Brag. 'I'm just telling my master it's time for our early morning walk. Wuff! Here he comes. I'm off!'

'Oh, dear,' sighed Drew. 'No one will teach me to hoot, after all. But, goodness, who is that?'

A splendid bird stood on top of the henhouse. On his head he wore a red comb, like a king's crown. His feathers gleamed like silk and he had the most magnificent curling tail feathers.

'Good morning, SIR,' said Drew, very politely. 'Who are you?'

'Good morning, little owl,' the big bird replied. 'I'm King, the cockerel. And now it is daylight, I must make sure everyone is awake.'

King the cockerel threw back his head and crowed.

'Cock-a-doodle-doo-ooo!'

It was the loudest, most splendid voice little Drew had ever heard.

'Itty ooo!' he hooted admiringly.

King stopped in the middle of another crow and stared at Drew.

'Itty what?' he asked. 'That's a weak and wobbly noise to be making!'

'But it's the best I can do-oo,' sobbed Drew. 'Boo-hoo. I wish I could sing like you-oo.'

'Cheer up,' said King briskly. (He was rather a show-off and loved to be admired, so he rather liked Drew.) 'Cheer up, little owl. I'll teach you how to crow. Watch me, and listen carefully.' King stood on tiptoe, opened his beak wide and crowed, over and over again, until at last Drew understood just how it was done.

'Cock-a-whoodle-whoo!' he crowed, so loudly that he bounced right up in the air. He had to spread his wings so he could land safely on the henhouse roof beside King.

'Not bad. Not bad at all,' King told him. 'Well, it's time you went home, young owl. My word, your mother will be proud of you!'

So Drew flew home and crept into the nest beside Mrs Owl, Hugh, Sue and Pru, to sleep until the moon rose again that night.

Then his family had a surprise!

'Never,' said Mrs Owl, 'never have I heard such a wonderful, musical song. Sing it again, Drew.'

So Drew sang his song again, and has been singing it each night ever since.

If you should wake one night when it is still quite dark and hear 'Cock-a-whoodle-whoooo!'

don't worry. You can curl up and go cosily back to sleep, for it isn't King you can hear, calling that it's time to get up.

No, it's Drew the Owl, hooting his own special cry for you as he goes hunting in the moonlight across fields and woods and gardens. 'Cock-a-whoodle-whoooo!'

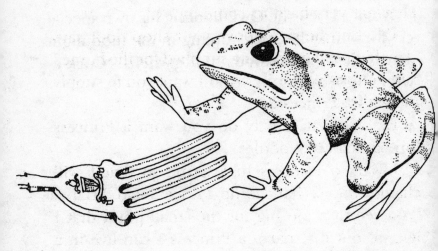

Frizby's royal invitation

Val Annan

Are you sitting comfortably? Then I'll begin.

Mr Noodles owned a shop in the market place. It was full of useful things like yellow buckets, shiny saucepans, black kettles, brown pots and wooden spoons.

One day, a tall green frog hopped into the shop.

'Good-day, Mr Noodles,' said the frog. 'My name is Frizby Frog and I would like a Princess please.'

28

Mr Noodles stared in amazement at the frog.

'Er ... I don't stock Princesses, I'm afraid. They are very hard to come by ...'

'Oh, but the sign above your shop door says 'Anything and everything supplied for the home,' said Frizby stubbornly. 'And I want you to supply me with a Princess!'

'Er ... what exactly do you want a Princess for?' asked Mr Noodles.

'I want a Princess to kiss me so that I will change into a handsome Prince!' said Frizby. 'You see, I'm too big for the small pond that I live in, but if I marry a Princess I can live in a Palace!'

'But what makes you think *you* will change into a handsome Prince?' asked Mr Noodles.

'Because I've just read a story. It was all about a tall green frog who is kissed by a Princess and the frog then turns into a handsome Prince.'

'But that sort of thing only happens to very special frogs,' said Mr Noodles.

'But I AM a very special frog!' said Frizby indignantly. 'My Mum tells everyone that I'm special!'

'Er ... perhaps you can come back tomorrow?' said Mr Noodles. 'A Princess might turn up – you never know your luck.'

And indeed a Princess did turn up, just ten

minutes after Frizby Frog had left Mr Noodles' shop! As she went into the butcher's shop next door, Mr Noodles noticed the silver crown on her head. Mr Noodles followed her.

There he found the butcher bowing very humbly. 'Can I interest you in a piece of beef, Your Highness? Or a nice leg of lamb, perhaps?' he said.

The Princess turned up her nose.

'No! No! No! I want something *unusual* to eat. We are *always* having beef or roast lamb!'

'Tripe!' said the butcher. 'Tripe is a most unusual royal dish. Boil it up with some milk and onions and it's fit for a King, Queen or Princess!'

'Oh, very well! I'll try some tripe,' sighed the Princess.

As she was leaving the butcher's, Mr Noodles said nervously: 'Er – s'cuse me, Your Highness . . . but can I interest you in a nice green frog?'

'Can you interest me in a nice green frog!' she said. 'Is he a nice *big* frog?'

'Oh, quite the biggest and tallest frog I've ever seen!' said Mr Noodles.

'Is he young and tender?' asked the Princess.

'Oh, I'm sure he is!' said Mr Noodles.

'Good!' said the Princess. 'Deliver him to the Palace tomorrow for lunch!'

'Oh, yes, Your Highness!' said Mr Noodles.

So, when Frizby Frog turned up the next morning he was delighted when Mr Noodles said, 'I'm to take you to the Palace for lunch!'

'Oh, good!' said Frizby Frog. 'I wonder what we'll have to eat? I've never had a Royal Invitation before!'

So Mr Noodles and Frizby Frog went to the Palace. They rang the silver bell on the silver gates.

'Come round to the kitchen door!' yelled the Princess.

'Well, really!' said Frizby Frog. 'I don't think much of her manners – fancy sending a guest to the kitchen door! I don't think she's a very NICE Princess!'

'Er . . . you didn't ask for a nice one,' said Mr Noodles.

And when the Princess opened the back door, Frizby Frog didn't like the look of her at all. It wasn't that she wasn't beautiful or anything like that but she had a nasty gleam in her eye when she looked at him. She pushed Mr Noodles away before he could introduce Frizby Frog.

'Send your bill through the post!' she said.

And then the rude Princess poked Frizby Frog with a big fork.

'Hmm,' she said. 'There's not much meat on these thin legs of yours.'

'Not much meat! Well, really! I haven't come

here to be insulted! I've had enough of this!'

And before the Princess could grab him, Frizby Frog leapt away. He ran after Mr Noodles.

'Oh, Frizby Frog! I think you've had a narrow escape,' said Mr Noodles. 'I do believe the Princess wanted to *eat* you!'

'Eat me!' said Frizby Frog. 'Nonsense! She wanted to kiss me so that I would turn into a handsome Prince and then she could marry me and nag me and push me around with a big fork for the rest of my life! NO THANK YOU! I'm going back to my nice green pond. I rather like being a big frog in a small pond after all!'

The little cat with the very long tail

Diana Webb

Are you sitting comfortably? Then I'll begin.

There was once a toy cat with a small round yellow body and a very very long, very very fat yellow tail. His tail was so long that it reached right to the end of the shelf in the shop where the little cat sat waiting for someone to buy him. All the other animals on the same shelf had to sit behind it.

'I don't know why you need such a long fat tail,' said the toy rabbit who sat next to him. 'It takes up too much room.'

33

'I don't know why you need such long ears,' said the little cat.

'But my ears aren't as long as all that,' said the rabbit. 'Your tail is ten times as long as one of my ears.'

'I can't help it,' said the little cat, who didn't understand why he had such a long tail either, when he could see that all the other cats in the shop had quite short tails. 'Perhaps I shall find out one day why I have such a long fat tail.'

'Maybe people could balance on it like a tightrope in a circus,' suggested a toy elephant.

'Maybe,' said the little cat, but he didn't really like the idea of people walking on his tail.

'Maybe one end of it could be tied to the branch of a tree and people could climb up it like a pole,' said a toy monkey.

'Maybe,' said the little cat, but he didn't really like the idea of people climbing up his tail.

'Maybe people who wanted to cross a river could throw it across the water and use it as a bridge,' said a toy duck.

'Maybe,' said the little cat, but he didn't really like the idea of people using his tail as a bridge. It might get wet.

'Maybe people will just trip over it and get cross,' said the rabbit. 'If you ask me you should have it shortened.'

'No,' said the little cat. 'I don't think I should

do that. I'm sure there must be a good reason why my tail is the way it is.'

Then one day a lady came into the shop. She bought the little cat with the very long tail and she bought the rabbit next to him as well. When she got home she gave the rabbit to her little boy as a present but she took the little cat with the very long tail and put him down by the door to the living room as far away from everyone as she could.

The little cat felt sad.

At night when the little boy was going to bed he dropped his new rabbit by the door. The rabbit laughed at the little cat with the long tail.

'That lady knows now that buying you was a mistake. I expect she's put you by the door to remind her to take you to a jumble sale next time she goes out. But I don't think anyone else would be silly enough to buy something with such a stupid long tail, even at a jumble sale.'

The little cat said nothing, but he was very unhappy.

After the lady had put her little boy to bed she came back into the room and shut the door. She picked up the little cat with the very long tail and sat him at one end of the door. Then she stretched out his tail all along the carpet in front of the bottom of the door. The little cat felt very comfortable with his tail stretched along the bottom of the door. It fitted there very well.

Outside the house the wind was blowing hard. It blew through the gap under the front door into the hall. It blew through the gap under the kitchen door into the kitchen. It blew through the gap under the dining room door into the dining room. It tried to blow through the gap under the living room door into the living room but it couldn't because the little cat's tail was in the way.

The little cat felt the wind pushing against his tail and suddenly he knew why his tail was so long and fat.

'Of course,' he said to himself. 'It's to stop the wind blowing under the door into the room, so the people inside don't catch cold.' And he was extremely happy.

The wind tried very hard to push its way into the room but the little cat's tail was so long and so fat that the wind couldn't get past no matter how hard it blew.

'I always knew I should find out one day why I had such a very special kind of tail' said the little cat. He looked at the rabbit's short stubby tail. 'It's only a very special kind of tail that can keep out something as big and strong as the wind!'

Chick, Chicklet and Chick-a-Ling

Ivy Eastwick

Are you sitting comfortably? Then I'll begin.

'Hurry! hurry!' said Mrs Hen. 'Come along out now. All of you.'

The three little eggs stayed as they were.

Eggs.

Just eggs.

Not a chirp.

Not a cheep.

Just three brown-shelled eggs.

'It's time,' called Mrs Hen. 'It's Spring. Come along out!'

The three little eggs stayed as they were.

Eggs.

Just eggs.

Not a chirp.

Not a cheep.

Just three brown-shelled eggs.

'I have sat here too long. Come on. The sun is shining,' said Mrs Hen.

The three little eggs stayed as they were.

'The sky is blue. Oh, so very blue,' said Mrs Hen. 'Will nothing bring you out?'

The three little eggs stayed as they were.

'The worms are moving around under the ground. They are waiting for you,' said Mrs Hen.

There was a sound from one egg.

Tap.

There was a sound from the second egg.

Tap. Tap.

There was a sound from the third egg.

Tap. Tap. Tap.

'And about time too!' said their mother. A little downy yellow head peeped out of one shell.

'Hello, Mother,' he chirped.

'Hello, Chick,' said his mother.

A second yellow head peeped out of the second shell.

'Hello, Mother,' he chirped.

'Welcome, Chicklet,' said his mother.

38

The third yellow head broke through his shell. He looked all round him. Up. And down.

'Where are the worms?' he asked. 'Where is the blue sky? Where is the sun?'

His mother looked up and down too. The sky was grey. The sun had gone.

'I'm going back,' said the third little chick crossly. 'I'm going back into the shell. There isn't any sun. There isn't any blue sky. And there are no worms!'

He stamped his foot angrily. Then he kicked the eggshell out of the nest.

'You can't go back, Chick-a-Ling,' said his mother. 'The eggshell is broken.'

'I don't care,' said Chick-a-Ling. 'I am going back. And I shall wait there until the worms come up, the sun comes out and the sky turns blue.'

And he stomped back into his eggshell.

'Oh, dear,' said his mother. 'What a tiresome chick this one is. How can I help it if the weather changes and the worms hide?'

It began to rain.

'Come under my wing,' said Mrs Hen. Chick and Chicklet hopped under their mother's wing.

Chick-a-Ling stayed where he was – in the open-topped shell.

'You'll get wet,' said his mother.

39

'Don't care,' said Chick-a-Ling.

'Please come, Chick-a-Ling,' said Chicklet.

'Do come, Chick-a-Ling,' said Chick.

'NO!' Chick-a-Ling answered. 'I'll wait here, till the sky turns blue and the sun comes out and the worms come up from the ground.'

There was a bright flash of lightning.

'What's that?' asked Chick-a-Ling.

'It's lightning,' said his mother.

'I don't like lightning,' said Chick-a-Ling.

'Then come under my wing and you won't see it,' said his mother.

'NO!' said Chick-a-Ling.

There was a loud crash of thunder.

'What's that?' asked Chick-a-Ling.

'It's thunder,' said his mother.

'I don't like thunder,' said Chick-a-Ling.

'Then come under my wing and you won't hear it,' said his mother.

'No!' said Chick-a-Ling.

'You'll get very wet out there,' said his mother.

'Don't care,' said Chick-a-Ling.

'You'll catch cold,' said his mother.

'Don't care,' said Chick-a-Ling.

Chick and Chicklet were dry and warm under their mother's wing. Soon Chick-a-Ling was drenched. His feathers hung limp. His little feet were cold. His little eyes began to run with water. He shivered.

'Please, Chick-a-Ling, dear little Chick-a-Ling, come under my wing.' his mother pleaded.

But he was stubborn.

'No,' he said.

'Well, then, *I* must come to *you*,' she said, and she walked out of the nest to where Chick-a-Ling stood shivering in his eggshell. She put her wing over him and then she clucked to her other two chicks who came and sheltered under her other wing.

She said: 'You'll soon be dry, Chick-a-Ling.'

Chick-a-Ling shivered under her wing. Then he grew a little warmer and a little drier and his eyes stopped watering and he stopped shivering. 'Mother is right,' he thought. 'It is better here than out there in the rain, with the lightning and the thunder.'

He stayed there for ten minutes. Then he heard his mother call: 'You may come out now, my little ones. The rain has nearly stopped and the sun is out.'

Chick came hopping out.

Chicklet came hopping out.

But Chick-a-Ling said: 'No. I'd rather stay here.'

'Oh, Chick-a-Ling,' said his mother. 'Come out and see how pretty the world can be.'

'No,' said Chick-a-Ling.

He heard Chick and Chicklet talking together. They were saying things like: 'Sweet. Sweet. Pretty-sweet. Pretty-sweet. Cheep-sweet. Sweet-cheep.'

He poked his head out from under his mother's wing.

He looked up at the sky.

It was blue.

He looked up at the sun.

It was golden.

AND there was a beautiful SOMETHING in the sky.

The SOMETHING was shaped like a bow.

A HUGE bow.

It was blue and mauve and pink and green and yellow.

'Mother! Mother! Look!' cried Chick-a-Ling. 'Up there! What is it?'

His mother looked and then she laughed.

'It is the April Rainbow, Chick-a-Ling,' she told him.

'I LIKE rainbow, Mother,' said Chick-a-Ling, and he stepped right out of his shell.

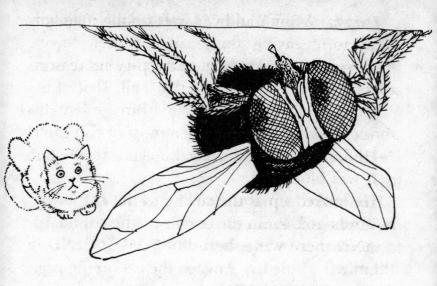

Little fly on the ceiling

Angela Pickering

Are you sitting comfortably? Then I'll begin.

The little fly was walking on the ceiling. From the corner by the door to the corner by the window. From the corner by the window to the corner by the door.

'Little fly, little fly,' yawned the cat on the rug, 'why do you walk on the ceiling?'

The little fly walked across the ceiling to the lampshade. He hung upside down by his sticky feet and looked at the cat on the rug.

43

'Zzzzzz. Why shouldn't I walk on the ceiling if I want to?'

'No reason,' said the cat on the rug, 'no reason at all. I just wondered why, that's all. *Most* of us walk on the ground.'

'Ah,' said the little fly. 'Then most of you can't see the table, Grandpa's table laid ready for tea.'

He walked across the ceiling to the corner by the cupboard. From the corner by the cupboard to the corner by the shelf.

'Little fly, little fly,' yawned the cat on the rug, 'that's not a reason. Grandpa would never invite you for tea. Why, tell me why, do you walk on the ceiling?'

'Zzzzzz. Why shouldn't I walk on the ceiling if I want to?'

'No reason,' said the cat on the rug, 'no reason at all. I just wondered why, that's all. *Most* of us walk on the ground.'

'Ah,' said the little fly, 'then most of you can't see Grandpa's pot plants growing on the sill.'

He walked across the ceiling. From the corner by the shelf to the corner by the cupboard. From the corner by the cupboard to the corner by the shelf.

'Little fly, little fly,' yawned the cat on the rug, 'that's not a reason. Grandpa's plants will grow no matter how high you are. Why, tell me why, do you walk on the ceiling?'

'Zzzzzz. Why shouldn't I walk on the ceiling if I want to?'

'No reason,' said the cat on the rug, 'no reason at all. I just wondered why, that's all. *Most* of us walk on the ground.'

'Ah,' said the little fly, 'then most of you can't see the top of Grandpa's shiny head. Such a smooth bald head it is. No hair left at all. I would like to settle on Grandpa's shiny head.'

'Little fly, little fly,' yawned the cat on the rug, 'that's not a reason. Grandpa would never let you settle on his shiny bald head. Why, tell me why, do you walk on the ceiling?'

'Ah,' said the little fly, 'so many questions. Do you really want to know why I walk on the ceiling?'

'Well,' yawned the cat, 'it's what I keep asking.'

The little fly walked across the ceiling. From the corner by the shelf to the corner by the door. From the corner by the door to the very very middle. Right over the mat where the cat was sitting.

'Zzzzzz,' said the little fly. 'I walk on the ceiling so that Grandpa's cat cannot swot me with his paw. Zzzzzz. That's why!'

45

And then the little fly sang this song:

The Little Fly's Song

I get a kind of feeling
When I'm walking on the ceiling
That the cat is waiting for me down below.
My head is kind of reeling
When I'm walking on the ceiling,
I am better up, and down I will not go.
I would rather not be squealing
On the mat. For on the ceiling
Is the safest place of all I surely know.
I've a squealing kind of feeling,
And a reeling kind of feeling,
And a wheeling kind of feeling,
When I'm walking on the ceiling,
For the cat is waiting for me down below.

Hugo the hippo sings

Rachel Ford

Are you sitting comfortably? Then I'll begin.

Hugo the hippo lived in the jungle. He had no reason to be unhappy, but he was. He was unhappy because he could not sing. Every night without fail, he would dream of being a great opera singer. He would sing at the Albert Hall and everyone would applaud and cheer. He would be dressed in a top hat and tails. He would have a beautiful black velvet bow-tie.

Every morning when Hugo woke up, he would feel so disappointed, because none of it was true. It was just a dream.

One starlit night, just as Hugo was saying his prayers, a very bright star caught his eye. Then he remembered what his mother had told him when he was a baby hippo: 'If you ever see a very bright star shining in the sky you must make a wish, but you must not tell anyone what you have wished for.'

So Hugo closed his eyes tightly and made a wish. And then he fell asleep.

While Hugo slept the star came down and said, 'Hugo dear, your wish shall be granted.'

The next morning when Hugo woke up, he opened his mouth to yawn and the most lovely sound came out of his mouth. He was so happy, he jumped around and laughed. He could sing! He decided he would have a party for all of his friends. He invited Stripes the tiger; Ellie the elephant; his best friend Joshua Mud, the hippo who lived next door; Lilly the lioness and Aunty Antelope.

Hugo had a troublesome time trying to get the party ready because hippos are large animals and tend to be rather clumsy. Once he put his foot in the jelly, slipped, and landed in the cake. But at last everything was ready. He put on his best jungle trousers and his very brightly coloured holiday shirt. Then his guests started to arrive. They were all dressed in their best clothes too.

Lilly the lioness was wearing a very fetching pink frilly skirt. They had a wonderful time.

When they were all sitting around the table, Hugo stood up. In a very loud voice, he said, 'I can sing!'

The animals all looked at one another in amazement.

'Oh, no you can't, Hugo,' they said.

'But I *can*,' replied Hugo, 'and what's more, I will sing to you now.' Hugo started to sing. The animals couldn't believe their ears. Hugo was making the most beautiful sound.

Nearby in the jungle, some people were on a safari. When they heard this wonderful singing they just had to find out what it was. They carefully followed the sound of the music and found themselves at Hugo's home.

They knocked on the door and were rather surprised when it was opened by a lioness in a pink frilly skirt.

'Can I help you?' she asked.

'We are looking for the person who was singing so beautifully just a few minutes ago,' said one of the men.

'Oh, that's Hugo the hippo,' replied Lilly. 'He's over there.'

The men told Hugo of a talent competition that was being held the very next evening at the Albert Hall in London. Hugo was very excited.

They all got on an aeroplane and flew to London straight away, and the next night, Hugo the hippo found himself at the Albert Hall dressed in top hat and tails and wearing a black velvet bow-tie round his neck.

Hugo was the last one to go on stage before the judges decided who was to be the winner of the competition and he sang beautifully!

The judges loved his singing and they gave him full marks. Hugo was the winner! He was presented with a big gold cup full of strawberry jam sandwiches!

At last Hugo's dream had come true, and he was a world-famous opera singer.

The dustbin cat

May K. Randell

Are you sitting comfortably. Then I'll begin.

An enormous striped marmalade cat, who weighed as much as a bag of oranges, sat on the new dustbin lid. The lid shone in the sun. It was nice and warm, so the cat purred happily.

Small Black Dog lived across the road. HE was tied up to a shady tree. He wished he was a marmalade cat who could sit on a warm dustbin lid.

But it was a dustbin-emptying day! And along came the dust-cart. Rattle-clang-BANG!

51

Fred the dustman leapt off the dust-cart. He began to empty all the bins in the road. Small Black Dog didn't like the noise, so he began to bark and all the neighbourhood dogs joined in! There was a terrible din as the dustbins were flung down and lids crashed to the ground. Still the enormous marmalade cat, who weighed as much as a bag of oranges, didn't get off his dustbin lid.

Up came Fred the dustman.

'OFF! OFF YOU GET, ginger cat,' he yelled.

'Miaow-Merrow,' went the dustbin cat loudly, which meant: 'I WON'T!'

Small Black Dog ran down as far as his rope would let him. He laughed and laughed. 'Arf! Arf! Arf!' Fred placed his hands on his hips. He stuck out his jaw and made a terrible face at the marmalade cat.

Then he said very softly, 'If you don't clear off that dustbin lid NOW, I'm going to have to push you off!'

But the cat only sat tight and spread himself all over the dustbin lid. Then he sharpened his claws on the edge of it, which made the dustman howl!

'Yee-ow, Merrow, Mee-ow!' the marmalade cat went, which meant: 'Just you try anything, mate, and see what happens to you . . .'

Small Black Dog was enjoying himself watching. He laughed until tears ran down the end of his little wet black nose.

'Arf! Arf! Arf! Arf! ARF!' he went, and all the other dogs in the neighbourhood, although THEY didn't know what was going on, laughed too!

Then Fred shouted across to his driver: 'Turn off the engine a minute, Joe. We've got us a fat, stubborn, old, ginger cat here, who won't get off this dustbin lid.'

'Why don't you push him off then, Fred?' called the driver.

But when Fred put out a hand, the enormous, striped, marmalade cat, who weighed as much as a bag of oranges, hissed and spat, and then ruffled and fluffed up all his fur. He waved his tail angrily. He got out all his sharpened claws. He was ready for anything!

'YOWL! ROWL! YOWL!' he went, which meant: 'I shall NOT get off this dustbin lid until *I* am ready!'

'You awful old cat!' cried Fred the dustman. 'Don't you know I have *got* to empty this dustbin? Get off that lid before I – '

'BIN! BIN! BIN! BI-IN! Breakfast time!' A nice, kind voice floated up the drive.

'BI-IN! *Please* hurry, Bin!' it called. And the enormous, striped, marmalade cat slid off the shiny dustbin lid and hurried away to get his breakfast.

'Well, I never! What a funny name for a cat! BIN!' said Fred, taking off his cap and mopping his forehead, and he quickly emptied the new dustbin.

Then Small Black Dog went back up his garden to dig up a breakfast bone and the dust-cart drove off up the hill, with a Brrrrrum-brrrm-clang-bang!

And when Bin the marmalade cat had finished his breakfast, he came back again to sit on the dustbin lid. The lid shone in the sun and the dustbin cat purred happily and went to sleep.

Mr Herbert Herbert's holiday

Margery Goulden

Are you sitting comfortably? Then I'll begin.

What's grey, has four legs, a tail and a trunk? No, it's not an elephant. It's a mouse going on holiday. And one mouse in particular. Mr Herbert Herbert. This is what happened.

'I've decided where to go,' said Mr Herbert Herbert, coming out from behind the central heating boiler waving a glossy holiday brochure in his paws.

I was very relieved. He'd been behind the

boiler with the brochure so long I'd begun to think I'd never see him again. Not a happy thought when I'd just bought a whole new red cannonball Edam cheese just for him.

'I'm going to Costa del Mouse,' he declared, and immediately began to pack. 'It's time I saw the world.'

'How will you get there?' I asked, pressing a thumb onto the lid of his trunk so that he could lock it. (Like everyone going on holiday, he'd packed too much.) 'Can I give you a lift?'

'No, thank you,' he said. 'I'll just hop on a number nineteen bus.'

And he did.

The house was very quiet without Mr Herbert Herbert, like your house is when you're at playgroup. Lovely, I thought. The whole place to myself! How I'd enjoy it. No squeak in the ear to wake me up an hour sooner than I wanted to wake up. No paw to switch off my favourite television programme so that Mr Herbert Herbert could watch Monster Mouse on the other channel. No demands for 'more Edam cheese' just when I was up to my ears in bubbles in the bath. Nobody to tear my newspaper, nibble my apples, spill my coffee, step on the toothpaste (with the top off) or, worst of all, gallop over the piano keys whenever the mood took him, yelling:

I'm happy when I'm singing,
I'm happy when I dance,
I'm happy happy as can be,
The song and dance mouse, that's me!

Of course, there's a lot more to his song than that. I call it the song without end. And if you've ever heard a mouse sing you'll know just how dreadful it sounds and just how beautifully peaceful the house was without Mr Song and Dance Mouse.

There was quiet and I loved it.

I did. Didn't I?

I must. I had what I wanted. Everything quiet. Everything to myself. My newspaper. My apples. My coffee. The bathroom. The television. The piano. Most especially the piano. But, oh, dear! How quiet the piano suddenly seemed. I don't play. Mr Herbert Herbert is the musical one. And there it stood. Silent.

It was then, looking at the piano, that I realized the truth. I missed Mr Herbert Herbert. I was lonely without him. I didn't want quiet. I didn't want the house, or anything, to myself. I wanted Mr Herbert Herbert back home and I still had another whole week alone. He'd gone to the Costa del Mouse for a fortnight.

I went into the kitchen and sat, very quietly, reading my newspaper and drinking my coffee, wishing Mr Herbert Herbert were there. Then I heard the rattle of the letterbox in the hall. A jolly, sunny, wish-you-were-here postcard from Mr Herbert Herbert no doubt, I thought, miserably. But it wasn't.

I was just in time to see Mr Herbert Herbert's trunk, even fuller than before, thud down onto the hall carpet. It was followed by Mr Herbert Herbert himself, complete with sombrero.

'Hasta la vista!' he said. That's 'goodbye' in Spanish, the language they speak on the Costa del Mouse. He'd meant to say 'hello' of course, but he'd only been there a week so I thought it a very good try. It was nearly right.

'Hello,' I said. 'Back so soon? How was the Costa del Mouse? How was the world?'

'There was no Edam cheese,' he said. 'And no piano.'

'Oh!' I said. 'So that's why you're back so soon.'

'No,' he said, trotting off to the back of the central heating boiler. 'I missed you. Did you miss me?'

I gave him the largest supper of Edam cheese he'd ever had in his life, and then I said, 'Won't you play the piano for me – please, Mr Herbert Herbert? And sing?'

And he did.

Wriggly Worm and the new pet

Eugenie Summerfield

Are you sitting comfortably? Then I'll begin.

One lazy day in June, Wriggly Worm was lying in the long grass enjoying the scent of flowers all round him. Anthea Ant came bustling along.

'Ah, there you are, Wriggly,' she said, 'I've something important to say to you.'

'Yes?' said Wriggly.

Anthea settled down beside him. 'I'm worried about Cirencester,' she began.

'Oh, not again!' groaned Wriggly. Cirencester, the sad stick insect, was a constant problem.

'How can anyone stop him from being sad for very long?'

'Ah-ha!' said Anthea, looking pleased with herself, 'I think I know the answer to that question.'

'You do?' Wriggly was glad to hear this.

'He's sad,' went on Anthea, 'because he needs someone to love him. And someone he can love too.'

'But, Anthea, we're his friends. We love him,' said Wriggly.

'Yes, yes, I know, but it's not the same as having someone or something of his very own.'

Then Wriggly Worm had a wonderful idea. 'What Cirencester needs is a pet,' he said.

Anthea wasn't so sure at first. She had never heard of a stick insect having a pet. She asked Wriggly Worm, 'What kind of a pet should it be, Wriggly? He'll need something quiet and friendly?'

Wriggly Worm went down into his secret tunnel to have a think about this. Then up he came, all excited.

'I've got it, Anthea! Leave it to me. I'll find Cirencester a nice quiet pet he can love.'

Anthea was delighted. 'Thank you, Wriggly. You are wonderful,' she said. 'Now I must go. I've got so much else to do.'

Wriggly Worm knew where there was a lost

pet who would just suit Cirencester. And as soon as Wriggly had found it, he sent it round to Cirencester right away.

So, later on, it was no surprise to Wriggly Worm when a note arrived by pigeon post which said: 'Please come to a special picnic today to meet my new pet. Lots of lettuce for tea. Love Cirencester. P.S. And thank you, Wriggly.'

Everybody had had notes by pigeon post that day. Sloppy Slug, Brown Snail, all the little Brown Snails, and Anthea Ant had all been invited. The little Brown Snails were all smart and shiny, ready for the picnic. Sloppy Slug was looking forward to lettuce for tea. He hoped it wouldn't all be eaten up before he got there. 'I think we'd better hurry,' he said. 'We don't want to be late for tea.'

'Wriggly,' said Brown Snail, as they crawled along together, 'what sort of a pet will it be?'

'Ah! yes, well . . . ' said Wriggly, because he knew. 'You'll have to wait and see.'

All the way along the little Brown Snails played guessing games. They were trying to find out what Cirencester's pet could be.

'It couldn't be an ant or an elephant.'

'It couldn't be a quail or a little Brown Snail.'

'Could it be a squirrel, with a big bushy tail?'

'Tell us, Wriggly. Tell us what it'll be.'

'No, no, no! You wait and see. Whatever it is, it will make Cirencester happy.'

Everyone was pleased about that. So, what a shock they all got when they reached Cirencester's special part of the garden and found him crying.

'Oh, woe, woe is me! Oh, why do sad things always happen to *me*? Oh, woe, oh, woe!'

Wriggly Worm hurried forward.

'Whatever's the matter, Cirencester?' he asked. 'We didn't expect to find you in tears.'

There was Cirencester sitting hunched up on a huge smooth brown stone, sobbing. 'I've lost him! I've lost my new pet,' he cried.

'We'll look for him,' said Wriggly. 'Everybody look for Cirencester's new pet.'

'Yes, yes,' cried all the little Brown Snails. They began to scurry hither and thither.

Then one called out, 'Wriggly, tell us what we're looking for?'

'Well,' Wriggly replied, 'his name's Shy. He's brown and smooth and rather like that huge thing Cirencester's sitting on –' He stopped suddenly. Then he said, 'Cirencester! You old silly, you're sitting on your new pet tortoise. You haven't lost him at all!'

Cirencester jumped down and hopped round to one end where there was quite a pile of lettuce leaves. A head came out of the shell and said in a whisper, 'Hello, I'm Shy.' And then popped back in again.

'He's very friendly really,' explained Cirencester, 'when he gets used to people.'

And he was. He gave the little Brown Snails rides on his back. He told them tortoise stories they had never heard before. They all had a lovely picnic. Everyone enjoyed it, especially Cirencester.

Nozzle the ant-eater

Christopher Newby

Are you sitting comfortably? Then I'll begin.

Nozzle is an ant-eater who lives in a small town. His cleverest friend is a bright red elephant called Horatio, who spends most of his spare time in the local swimming pool.

One day, when they were talking together, Horatio asked, 'Have you ever caught an ant, Nozzle?'

'No, I've never even thought about it,' replied Nozzle. 'Why do you ask?'

'Well, you are called an ant-eater,' said Horatio,

'but you are so nice I can't really imagine you eating ants.'

And as Horatio spoke, Nozzle suddenly thought: Horatio is right. I am *called* an ant-eater. I ought to be able to catch ants, and I've never even tried. Without saying another word, he left Horatio paddling in the pool and made his way to Hazelnut Wood, to catch his very first ant.

He had been looking for nearly an hour and was getting very fed up by his lack of success, when he heard a little voice.

'Hello, Nozzle,' it called, 'what are you doing?'

To his amazement Nozzle saw that it was his friend Cyril the ant talking.

'Don't move!' shouted Nozzle. 'I'm coming to catch you.'

Cyril looked surprised.

'But Nozzle, it's me! Cyril! your friend!' he exclaimed.

'But *I'm* an *ant-eater*,' announced Nozzle, trying to look fierce.

'You wouldn't eat me!' Cyril laughed. And with that, he ran down a rabbit burrow. Nozzle followed, putting his long nose right into the hole. Cyril carried on running, quite sure that Nozzle was only playing. Nozzle pushed harder, but he could not reach Cyril, who had now run right through the burrow and out to the other side. 'I'm over here, Nozzle,' he teased, enjoying the game more and more. Feeling rather annoyed, Nozzle tried to pull his nose out of the hole. It was then that he realized he was stuck. That made Cyril laugh even more. 'That should teach you not to chase your friends,' he said.

'I'm completely stuck!' said Nozzle. 'Please help me.'

'Well,' said Cyril, suddenly starting to feel sorry for Nozzle, 'I'd like to help, but I'm not strong enough to pull you out by myself. I'll go and look for Horatio the elephant.'

'Please be quick,' said Nozzle.

After only five minutes, Cyril found Horatio paddling in the swimming pool.

'Hello, Horatio,' he called. 'Can you come and help Nozzle please?'

'Of course,' smiled Horatio. 'What's the trouble?'

Cyril told him all about Nozzle's accident. Soon they were both hurrying back to Hazelnut Wood.

'Are you still stuck, Nozzle?' asked Horatio.

'Yes,' whispered Nozzle, who was now feeling rather ashamed of himself for chasing Cyril.

Carefully, Horatio wrapped his trunk around Nozzle's tail, and pulled. Nothing happened.

Horatio pulled again, and this time, his nose moved just a little. One more pull, and 'Pop' – out it came.

'Thank you, Horatio,' said Nozzle quietly, 'and, Cyril, I'm sorry I chased you. I'll never chase an ant again even if I am an ant-eater.'

And that is why, from that day to this, Nozzle has never eaten a single ant. Cyril is now one of his very best friends.

The warthog and the unicorn

Sandra Hannaford

Are you sitting comfortably? Then I'll begin.

Sometimes Warthog wished he had never found out how ugly he was, or that the tiger who had first told him he was had simply eaten him instead. He remembered how Tiger had snarled and swished his tail. 'What a horrid sight!' he had laughed.

'I beg your pardon, sir,' hiccuped Warthog, who had been eating roots. 'What is a horrid sight?'

'You are!' the tiger roared. 'If I were twice as hungry as I am I wouldn't put my smallest tooth in you. You're just too ugly to eat!'

He left Warthog hiccuping, 'You can't mean me! I'm not that ugly. I'm not!'

But he was. He would stand and look at himself in the pool and see his big flat nose and the whiskers on his chin; his warts like currants on a bun and teeth like piano keys; his red eyes squinted inwards and his ears stuck outwards and his belly touched the ground. And he would whisper to himself. 'It's true. I am too ugly to be seen.'

Now the King of the forest in those parts was a magic horse, a unicorn. He was blazing white with silver hooves and a single golden horn.

One day the King came down to the river alone to drink, and halted in surprise. For there on the river bank was a hole; and in the hole was mud; and in the mud was an animal the King had never seen before, making the most appalling din. Deep in the mud it snorted and roared, gulped and splashed, squelched and sucked and slurped. And all the time it sang to itself making noises like a train. The King crept closer to watch.

It was, of course, Warthog in the hole and all at once he opened his eyes and saw the King.

'Oh, hello,' he said, 'Nice day. Hot. Do you

want some mud?'

'I beg your pardon?' said the King.

'Some mud.' Warthog thought he should explain. 'This is mud. Wonderful stuff. Cool yer. Fun.' And to show the King what fun it was he stood on his head and lay on his back and surged and sploshed and ducked like a submarine, explaining all the time at the top of his voice until birds took off from the trees a mile downstream.

'Try it yourself!' Warthog cried.

'I don't really think that –' said the King; but just as he spoke, he fell in.

Now a warthog's legs are short and thick, just right for mud; but a unicorn's are long and thin and quite wrong.

The mud got everywhere and Warthog didn't help. When he should have pushed, he pulled; and when he should have pulled, he pushed – very hard, until the King was covered in weeds and mud.

'Like it?' asked Warthog hopefully.

The King spat out some weeds and thought. Then he asked. 'Why do you like mud so much, my friend?'

'Because I can hide in it,' said Warthog. 'And no one can see how ugly I am.' He sighed.

'Does everyone call you ugly?' asked the King.

'They say I'm even too ugly to eat!' Warthog sobbed.

At this very moment out jumped Toad awakened from his sleep by the noise and swollen with rage.

'What! what!' he croaked. 'What do you mean by making that din? You spoil my sleep and spoil the view. I'll see you pay for this, splashing mud everywhere!'

Just then Toad realized there was something very familiar about the second warthog. 'Oh dear,' he squeaked, 'Your Majesty! How could I know it was your royal self?'

'Toad,' said the King, 'you are a snob. It should not have mattered whether you knew or not. Go and fetch all the animals in the forest and bring them here at once.'

So Toad set off more frightened than he had ever been before and soon every creature in the forest stood on the river bank before a King they had never seen so plastered with mud and hung with weed. And he looked very grim indeed.

'Now listen to me,' said the King. 'This is Warthog. You all frightened him so much by calling him a horrid sight, that he decided to live here in this hole covered with mud where none of you would see what you call his ugliness. Stand up, Warthog!'

'I am standing up, Your Majesty,' said Warthog,

deep in the mud and holding up the King.

'Very well,' said the King. 'Now, you animals, why do you call this good warthog an ugly beast? You, Rat, you tell me.'

'Well – ' said Rat, twitching his tail, and looking embarrassed.

'You, Tiger,' said the King, 'you tell me.'

'Aaaah, Your Majesty.' The tiger showed his teeth but couldn't say anything.

'He's different,' said Toad, very loudly, and wished at once he had not.

'Different?' asked the King. 'Different, Toad? You all are different, every one of you. If being different means being ugly then all of us are ugly too. Stand up, Warthog!' said the King again.

'I AM standing up, your Highnessty,' Warthog groaned, still not very sure of what was going on.

The King frowned terribly in case anyone should laugh. 'You have all been snobs,' he told the animals. 'You left poor Warthog here alone and let him cover himself with mud because he is different from you all. And here I found him, an animal more honest, kind and gentle than any one of you. Henceforth,' said the King, 'Warthog will live at Court. He will take his place – '

'Your Majesty!' Warthog tried to interrupt.

' – in every procession,' continued the King.

72

'Your Majesty,' Warthog tried again, 'I'd rather stay here, if you please.'

'But why?' asked the King.

'Because of the mud,' Warthog explained. 'And this hole of mine, you see, is home.'

'I see,' said the King. 'Then this is my command. All of you here will come every day to Warthog's hole to talk to him.'

And so from that day onwards Warthog never lacked for friends and no one ever told him he was ugly again. And the King came once a week as well, to try the mud (or so he said), and to talk with his good friend.

Just a bad day

Rosalie Eisenstein

Are you sitting comfortably? Then I'll begin.

Badger woke up early. For some reason he just did not feel right. He did not want to get up, yet he did not feel like sleeping either. He humped and bumped around under the covers. Every so often he heaved enormous sighs. At last he decided to get up.

He made breakfast and sat munching toast and strawberry jam. He had received the jam as a present, the day before. He had looked forward to breakfast so he could taste it. It was quite delicious but he did not enjoy it.

Hoggy arrived not long afterwards.

'Are you ready?' he asked.

'Ready for what?' said Badger rudely.

'I thought we had decided to take a walk this morning,' said Hoggy.

'Oh, I'm not in the mood,' said Badger. 'In fact I am in a thoroughly bad mood today,' he added.

'Perhaps you are ill,' said Hoggy. 'You don't look ill though. In fact you look quite well. Yes, you look very well," he continued, 'except you do look cross. Perhaps you are ill after all.'

'I am not ill,' shouted Badger, 'and I feel just fine. It's just a bad day.'

'Come for a walk anyway,' persuaded Hoggy. 'I am sure it will make you feel better.'

'Oh, all right,' grumbled Badger.

All through the walk he dragged along behind Hoggy. Whatever Hoggy said, Badger just grunted in reply, and he grumbled continually.

'I am tired.'

'I am hungry.'

'Oh, it is a bad day.'

He almost tripped over a tortoise who was crossing the path in front of him.

'Mind where you are going!' shouted Badger.

'I am terribly sorry,' said the tortoise.

'And so you should be,' replied Badger.

Hoggy was very surprised at Badger. 'He is in a bad mood,' he said to himself. 'Come back to my house,' he said to Badger. 'We will have tea. I baked a cake.'

Badger usually cheered up at the thought of tea but he continued grumbling as he followed Hoggy.

When they had sat down, Hoggy poured tea and put on a plate a round, golden cake. It smelt delicious.

'I only like chocolate cake,' complained Badger, helping himself to a slice. In all, he took three slices, so it must have been nice, but still looked decidedly cross.

They started doing a jigsaw together but Badger soon stood up and stretched. 'I don't feel like doing this jigsaw,' he said. 'Goodbye, I am going home.'

He went straight to bed when he got home, still in a very bad mood.

He awoke next morning feeling his usual self. He ran round to Hoggy's house clutching his jar of strawberry jam.

'I am sorry I was so cross yesterday, Hoggy,' he said. 'It was just a bad day.'

The secret
Kathleen Pateman

Are you sitting comfortably? Then I'll begin.

Richard loved going next door to see Miss Tippit because she had Henry. Henry was a big green parrot, in a shiny cage, who squealed and squawked all the day long. Richard couldn't understand a word it said, but Miss Tippit didn't seem to mind. She talked to Henry from morning till night-time, but still Henry only squawked back.

One day Richard was standing beside Henry's

cage, listening to him squealing, 'Waaak, waaaak, waaaaak!' and not understanding a word he was saying.

'I do wish you would talk properly,' he said, as he watched Henry clean the feathers under his wings. 'All you can say is 'Squawk, squawk.' Then Richard said to him in a very firm voice, 'Why don't you answer me, Henry, when I speak to you?'

Henry stopped scratching himself, and looked at Richard with his head on one side. Then suddenly he said, as plainly as you or I could have done, 'Why can't you fly?'

Richard just stared. He opened his mouth to answer, but Henry interrupted and said again, 'Why can't you fly, Richard Watts?'

Richard was more amazed than ever. 'He even knows my name' he thought, but he answered quickly, 'Because I haven't any wings, silly.'

'Well, I'm cleverer than you, then,' said Henry, ''Cos I can fly and talk. I am a very clever parrot. In fact, I must be the cleverest parrot in the whole world.' And he squealed and squawked with delight and scrambled up and down his cage and puffed out all his green and red feathers. Then after a minute or two, he said quite quietly, 'I can sing too. Can you sing?'

'I can a bit,' said Richard.

'Do you know "Polly Put the Kettle On"?' Henry asked.

'Yes, we sing that at school,' answered Richard.

'Shall we sing it together, then?' asked Henry, and he climbed down the side of his cage until he was quite close to Richard and together they sang 'Polly Put the Kettle On' right the way through.

'You have a very fine voice,' said Richard, when they had finished.

'I can recite too,' said Henry, and he recited 'I love little pussy, her coat is so warm,' without making a single mistake.

'That was very good,' said Richard. 'What else can you do?'

But Henry just looked hard at Richard, went to the topmost perch in his cage and went straight off to sleep.

Just at that moment Miss Tippit came into the room with a biscuit and a glass of orange juice for Richard.

'Been talking to my Henry, have you?' she said. 'He squawks all day long, but you can never understand a word he says.'

Henry, hearing this, opened one eye and winked at Richard and Richard winked back at Henry.

It was their secret, you see.

Well, you can't tell grown-ups everything, can you?

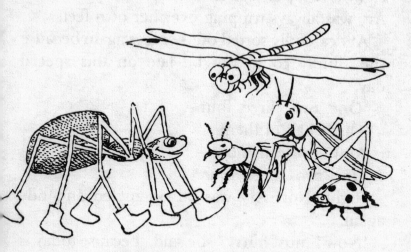

Ary the spider

Irene Holness

Are you sitting comfortably? Then I'll begin.

'Bump! Ouch! Bother! Ow!'

Ary Spider had fallen over. Again. But she mustn't be late today. She hadn't tripped over the broken twigs lying on the garden. She hadn't tripped over the long dry spikes of summer grass. She hadn't even tripped over the little nets of spiderweb her tiny cousins had woven on the lawn. No. Ary had tripped over her own feet. But she must not be late today.

There were a lot of feet to trip over too,

81

because Ary had a lot of legs. Eight legs. And it does not matter how quickly you count them, eight is a lot of legs and almost too many feet. Ary was always tripping over her own feet.

Ary carefully sorted out her legs again because she simply could not be late on this special day.

'One, two, three, four –
That's half of them.
And now four more –
One, two, three, four.'

Right. Now Ary was all untangled and tidy again.

'Now I must hurry,' she said, 'because today is a very special day and I really must not be late.'

She bustled along busily for a bit, scampering over stones, traipsing over twigs, running over the rockery and gallumping over the grass. Then she came to the smooth concrete path.

'Today is tremendously special,' she said to herself, 'and I must not be late. In fact I must be early.'

'Come on, eight legs, keep busy and whirling.'

Over the path she went at a great speed. Then it happened again.

'Bump! Ouch! Bother! Ow!'

Ary tripped over her own feet again and sat, all in a tangle, her legs all anyways whichways, on the path, feeling rather sad and sulky.

'It simply is not funny,
When one is in a hurry,
To have eight legs all tangled.
It keeps one's nerves quite jangled!'

She was speaking to Dotty the Ladybird who was passing on her way to somewhere very special.

'Never mind, Ary. Come along. You must not be late today, you know!'

'Yes, I know,' sighed Ary and sorted out her feet into order again.

'One, two, three, four,
Two behind and two before.
Now let me see – how many more?
One, two, three, four.'

She trundled on, along the garden path and over the garden path and past the birds' high concrete bath. Then, with a tangle of legs and a rush – under the flowery pink rose bush.

'Ary Spider, you are late!' chirruped Greg Grasshopper.

'You made us wait and wait and wait!' squeaked Bertie Beetle.

'But we won't scold you, not today!' smiled Dotty Ladybird.

'It's Ary's birthday! Hip, hooray!' piped up the butterflies, the dragon flies, the bumble bees and all Ary's friends who had gathered under the pink rose bush for her birthday party.

'Presents first,' said Bella Butterfly, and gave Ary a parcel tied up in a rose petal. Ary opened the parcel.

'Oh,' said Ary, in a very little voice (even for a spider), 'a pair of green shoes – just what I wanted.' But she couldn't help wondering what use were two shoes to a person with eight feet.

Then Bertie Beetle gave her a parcel. Ary opened it and inside was a pair of yellow shoes. 'Oh,' she said, 'just what I wanted.' But she couldn't help wondering what use were four shoes to a person with eight feet.

The next present was a pair of red shoes from Dotty Ladybird. 'I did need a pair of red shoes,' said Ary politely. Now she had six shoes – but she still had eight feet.

Delia Dragonfly's parcel was next. Inside was a pair of beautiful blue shoes.

'Ooo!' said Ary, 'I really truly did need a pair of blue shoes.' For now she had eight shoes for her eight feet.

'Put them on, Ary,' shouted all her friends. 'Green ones in front, then the yellow ones, then the red ones, and then the blue ones!'

So Ary put them on and very fine they looked.

'Now for some marching practice,' said Bertie Beetle.

'Attention! Green shoes! Quick march! Green, yellow, red, blue. Green, yellow, red, blue.'

'This is wonderful!' cried Ary. 'I know just which foot to put forward next. I'll never fall over my own feet again!'

And all her friends cheered and followed Ary as she marched happily down the long garden path.

Basil Brown, the fat cat

Richard Coughlin

Are you sitting comfortably? Then I'll begin.

Basil Brown was a ginger and white tom cat and he was fat. He was *much* too fat. His tummy swelled out at each side as if he'd swallowed a football. He was so fat, he could hardly move. People would point at him in the street and laugh at him and say: 'Ha! Ha! Look at that cat! How fat he is! He looks like a jelly on legs!'

Mrs Brown, Basil's owner, could not understand why he was so fat; she only ever gave him *enough* food, never too much.

'I'd better take him to the vet,' she said. 'Perhaps he's ill.'

Mrs Brown had a big cardboard box that she had brought her groceries home from the shops in, and into this box, she put the fat cat Basil and off to the vet they went.

'Hmmm,' said the vet, 'he *is* a fat cat, isn't he? Much too fat.'

'I can't understand it,' said Mrs Brown. 'I only ever give him just *enough* food, never too much.'

'Hmmm,' said the vet again. He examined Basil the fat cat carefully, prodding him here and there with his finger.

'Well,' he said at last, 'he's certainly not ill. I'm afraid there's nothing I can do. I just can't imagine why he is so fat.'

'Oh, well,' said Mrs Brown, and took Basil the fat cat home.

What could it be that made Basil Brown the fat cat so fat? It wasn't that Mrs Brown gave him too much food; she only ever gave him just *enough* food, never too much. It wasn't that he was ill; the vet had said that he certainly wasn't ill. Perhaps Basil the fat cat caught a lot of mice? No, that wasn't the reason he was so fat either; he was much too fat and slow to run after mice. What could the reason be, then? Why was Basil Brown the fat cat so fat?

This was Basil's secret: every night when it was dark and there was nobody about, he went quietly up and down the street where he lived, scavenging food from dustbins. There were a hundred houses on the street where Basil Brown the fat cat lived and that meant that there were a hundred dustbins. And in each one there were lots of good things for a cat to eat; things that people had thrown away. Things like pieces of fish, scraps of meat, chicken legs, even jam sandwiches and sometimes, Basil's favourite, chocolate sponge. It was a banquet fit for a king; and fit for a cat like Basil. So that was Basil the fat cat's secret and that's why he was so fat.

One night when the moon was shining brightly, Basil Brown the fat cat set out to see what he could find. He began with the dustbin belonging to the first house on the street. Standing on his hind legs he pushed the dustbin lid off with his nose. Then he heaved and puffed and panted and pulled his fat body into the bin.

'Ooh, look at all *this*!' he purred happily to himself for there, among the potato peelings and the soggy messy tea-leaves and all the messy, smelly stuff to be found in a dustbin, were four fishes' heads and a pickled onion.

'I can't understand why people throw such lovely food away,' purred Basil the fat cat, chewing and chomping greedily. 'I can't understand it at all, but I'm so glad that they *do* throw it away. Yummy *Yum*.'

When Basil Brown the fat cat had eaten all the fishes' heads and even the pickled onion in Number One's dustbin, he knocked the lid off the dustbin outside Number Two. Then he heaved and puffed and panted and pulled his fat body into the bin.

'Oh, look at all *this*,' he purred happily to himself. There, among the potato peelings and the soggy messy tea-leaves and all the messy, smelly stuff to be found in a dustbin, were six mouldy old sausages, half a corned beef sandwich and a doughnut.

'I can't understand why people throw such lovely food away,' purred Basil the fat cat, chewing and chomping greedily. 'I can't understand it at all, but I'm so glad that they *do* throw it away. Yummy yum.'

When Basil Brown the fat cat had eaten the six mouldy old sausages, the corned beef sandwich and the doughnut in Number Two's dustbin, he knocked off the lid of the dustbin outside Number Three. Then he heaved and puffed and panted and pulled his fat body into the bin.

'Ooh, look at all this!' he purred happily to himself. There, among the potato peelings and the soggy messy tea-leaves and the messy, smelly stuff to be found in a dustbin, were a piece of steak and kidney pie, a half eaten beefburger and an eccles cake with teeth marks on it.

'I can't understand why people throw such lovely food away,' purred Basil the fat cat, chewing and chomping greedily. 'I can't understand it at all, but I'm so glad that they *do* throw it away. Yummy yum.'

In and out of all the dustbins on the street went Basil Brown, the fat cat. In each bin, he found something good to eat and all the time he was getting fatter and fatter. At last, there was only one dustbin left; the one outside Number Ninety-nine, the house where Basil the fat cat lived.

'Mrs Brown's next,' said Basil the fat cat to himself. 'Mrs Brown's dustbin is my favourite. She nearly always throws away some of her delicious home-made chocolate sponge – just what I need to round off a jolly good night's hunting.'

Basil Brown the fat cat knocked the lid off Mrs Brown's dustbin. Then he puffed and panted and pulled his fat body into the bin.

'Ooh, look at all this!' he purred happily to himself. There, among the potato peelings and the soggy messy tea-leaves and all the messy, smelly stuff to be found in a dustbin, was a big slice of home-made chocolate sponge with a huge splodge of raspberry jam inside.

'I can't understand why people throw such

lovely food away,' purred Basil the fat cat, chewing and chomping greedily. 'I can't understand it at all, but I'm so glad that they *do* throw it away. Yummy yum.'

Basil Brown the fat cat was happy. He'd had a good night's eating and the chocolate sponge was scrumptious. But then something terrible happened. Mrs Brown came out of her house to put the empty milk bottles out and saw the lid of her dustbin lying on the ground. 'That's funny,' she said to herself. 'I'm sure I put that lid on before. Perhaps the wind blew it off.' Then she put the lid back on the bin very tightly indeed, so that it would not blow off again. She didn't know that Basil the fat cat was inside the bin.

Basil didn't notice that the lid had been put back on until he tried to get out. No matter how hard he tried, he could not get the lid off. When he realized what had happened, he became very frightened.

'Oh, help!' he wailed. 'Oh, help! Oh, please let me out! Oh, help me! Oh, please let me out!' But nobody could hear him. Basil Brown the fat cat had to stay in Mrs Brown's dustbin all night in the dark, among the potato peelings and the soggy messy tea-leaves and all the messy, smelly stuff to be found in a dustbin.

In the morning, some men came to empty all the bins in the street. A man called Bill lifted up

Mrs Brown's bin, with Basil inside it, and carried it to the big lorry to empty it.

'Crumbs,' said Bill, as he picked the bin up. 'This is a heavy one.' He took the lid off the bin and out jumped Basil Brown the fat cat with a frightened miaow and off he ran away down the street. Of course he couldn't run very quickly because he was so fat, but he ran faster than he had done for a long time.

'What a fat cat,' said Bill the dustbin man.

From that time on, Basil Brown never again went searching for food in dustbins and soon he became quite slim and handsome.

'That's because I only ever give him just *enough* food, never too much,' said Mrs Brown. But Basil Brown just smiled to himself.

The sheep who didn't count

Irene Holness

Are you sitting comfortably? Then I'll begin.

Cedric didn't count. Lambs often don't count and Cedric knew he didn't because everyone was always telling him so. He was one of twin lambs. The small one. The big one was Cecil. Cecil was superior. He counted. Sam the shepherd said so. Every evening when Sam and sheep dog Shap rounded up the flock on the hill and brought them down to the home field, Sam counted them: 'Snowy – one, Sandy – two, Sooty – three, Sally – four, Cecil – five, Cedric – oh, you're too little to count, Cindy – six . . .' and so on and so on, every single day. So Cedric knew he didn't count. He wasn't important at all.

Sometimes teachers from town schools brought their children to see the farm. The children liked all the animals but the smallest ones loved the sheep best because they were smaller than the cows and quieter than the pigs and didn't run away like the hens and their chicks. They were soft and warm and friendly to pat. They were easy to count.

One day Derek came to the farm with his class. Derek was new. He'd only just started school and he couldn't count very well yet.

He practised counting the sheep, giving each one a little pat.

'One, two, three, four – ' Then he saw Cedric. 'Oh, you're just a little one. I like you.' Derek patted Cedric and forgot all about counting.

Oh, dear, thought Cedric, small sheep are never counted.

Just then, a man arrived with a camera slung over his shoulder.

'Hello,' he said to the teacher. 'I'm from the *Meretown News*. I'd like some photographs of the children with the sheep for my paper, please.'

So the children lined up, the tallest at the back, shortest at the front, and some of the sheep lined up with them. The reporter took two pictures. Then he photographed some of the children patting the sheep.

'Right,' he said, 'I need one more picture. Let's have the three smallest children patting a sheep.'

'Good idea,' said the teacher. 'We'll have Angela, Barry and Derek.'

'Oh, but that won't do!' grumbled the reporter. 'I can't see the children properly. That big sheep takes up all the picture.'

Then Derek said, 'There is one little sheep in the flock.'

Cedric thought, Why, that's me! and skipped forward.

'Fine!' said the reporter. 'We need a sheep the same size as the children. That's what counts.'

So Cedric's picture was in the *Mereworth News*, with his name underneath.

'He's little,' everyone said, 'but he's nice, and that's what counts.'

Whenever schoolchildren visited the farm after that, they always looked out specially for Cedric. And Sam the shepherd always counted Cedric first: 'You're everyone's friend, Cedric,' he said. 'You really count now.'